USE TH
YOU

Kimberly Campanello

Paperback ISBN: 978-1-9997892-6-8

A CIP Catalogue Record
for this title is available from
the British Library.

Somesuch Editions
4 Wilkes Street
London E1 6QF
somesuch.co

Designed by *Guest Editions*
Typeset in *Alpina* by Grilli Type
Printed and bound by *Colt Press*
Printed on FSC certified paper

somesuch

L'histoire est déjà là, déjà inévitable, Celle d'un amour aveuglant, Toujours à venir, Jamais oublié.

Marguerite Duras, *L'Amant de la Chine du Nord*

Me voici sur la plage armoricaine.

Arthur Rimbaud, *Une saison en enfer*

The tent's zipper slaps her lightly. The breeze lifts the half-open flap then drops it at odd intervals on her bare back. Sometimes it's like a caress. Sometimes like something stronger. K doesn't move to avoid it. She might attract attention and so feel and therefore appear embarrassed. For now, she faces into the tent, her head turned slightly outward so as not to seem to ignore the conversation. Her long brown hair hangs over her chest. She wears underwear speckled with tiny pink roses.

The underwear package had contained a cardboard insert featuring a woman cut off just below her breasts and above her knees. The underwear hugs the woman's pelvis. No ripples in the fabric. The woman must have held her arms up for the photograph, or she has no arms. The woman's skin is free from bruises, scrapes, hair and moles. The woman's skin is peachy.

K's mother had bought these briefs for the trip: three packs, six pairs in each; folded, rolled into tubes and taped. Her mother had untaped, unrolled, unfolded and washed them. Then she'd dried them in the dryer, folded them in stacks and put them in the large green suitcase. That way K would have plenty of underwear.

There are no dryers over there, you know, her mother had said. You can't expect the mother to do laundry as often as me. Make sure you offer when yours builds up. Use a conditional sentence. If I did the laundry, it would be my pleasure.

Outside the tent, Rozenn is telling them, or really him – M – what she is going to do. Rozenn won't be staying. She will catch a ride home with her friends. Rozenn says that she shared her friend's tent last night because they, K and M, had abandoned her.

M is naked inside the tent, lying on his back. K thinks Rozenn can probably only see his legs from where she is positioned.

M doesn't sigh or argue that Rozenn should stay. He doesn't apologise.

The wind picks up the cool metal zip and traces it along K's spine.

Fine, M says, we'll stay. Ok, bye, see you, Rozenn says. They reply in unison, Bye, see you.

M rubs his eyes. K regards him as he falls asleep. She thinks about how his sister Rozenn had just been speaking to them while K was sitting like this, half naked in the tent doorway. How had this looked to her. How much had she seen. K doesn't have the desire to ask if things are alright or if this is strange.

There are clothes and lumps of bedding in the corners of the tent. It was so hot when the three of them packed that they had thrown just a couple of thin blankets into the trunk of M's car. They had mainly been concerned about space for food and boxes holding tiny bottles of beer. Nedeleg the dog had barked at their comings and goings from driveway to garage. K had packed the travellers jacket her mother had bought her from a mail order catalogue. Tie it around your waist to keep it handy. You never know when it might get chilly.

Rozenn would have guessed M was naked. Why hadn't he moved or gotten dressed when she called his name. Why hadn't K. What about the parents, what will they think when the trio doesn't return together. Will they come get the other two. That seems unlikely. M is an adult. His parents for this summer are K's 'parents'. They aren't going to drive out to force them home.

And what about the Honor Code. What about the Three Pillars. This sort of thing isn't spelled out, but it is implied. One of the Pillars is Host Family Experience.

The interview at the university last October to see how fluent K was. Madame Tanner's hair pulled back into a sharp bun, her skin taut over her elegant skull, her careful jewellery. A clipboard bearing K's application, a passport photo glued to the top of each section. Her arms and body cut off at the shoulders just above her breasts.

How fluent is K now.

What about classes next week. She will have to sit at a desk for five hours each day. Will she be sore, sitting like this. Will she want to tell Steph. Will she struggle to find the words to describe it. Will she want one specific word and end up having to talk around and around it, breaking it down into the graceless morsels of the only language available to her.

Like when she was trying to explain her brother's minor crash last spring during a family mountain biking trip to the other students. K had needed something simple – the flat tire. But she didn't know tire and didn't know flat in that particular sense. So the wheels were going then they were broken but not broken they were smashed but not smashed they were spread out. Not the wheels the thing around the wheels with the air in it. Soft and bouncy and then suddenly tired and run over like that grass over there by the tree. See the grass, see how it is not standing up, see how it is low. So was the thing that is the wheel but not the wheel that my brother had, the thing that made him fall.

My brother.

This 'brother'.

A hunger. A famine. Faim. Having a want. Envy. Envie

Words within words in this language she must speak.

K can't tell Audra, too Christian. Stephen is being sent home. Caught speaking English. One of the teachers is taking him to Paris this weekend to put him on a plane back to Indiana. This weekend, probably even right now, this morning, he's flying.

Who caught him. Who told.

K parses phrases using the words she has.

I'm a Catholic and I made a purity promise for a silver rose ring. It is hot. I am sore. I think that is ok. It fades. Good. I have hunger. I want.

M doesn't move. Now the wind won't move. No desire to get dressed. K lies down inside the tent.

I trace the air and the wind returns.

Their coach has arrived in Saint-Brieuc. The American stagiaires have been speaking French with each other for about seven hours now under the supervision of the teachers, who are native French speakers and PhD students from their state's university. No more English. French only. As per the contract they had signed, which came into force the moment the plane's wheels touched down. They managed through disembarkation, the border, bags and customs, the drive from Charles de Gaulle.

When their bus reaches the car park in Saint-Brieuc, the families are waiting. As each stagiaire steps down from the bus, a teacher calls out the name of the assigned family. K's foot touches the ground and the family name in her folder rings out. A man with a beard steps forward. The father. Armel. He kisses her on both cheeks and shakes the hands of the teachers. He seems surprised by the size of K's suitcase, which barely fits into the trunk of his car. Her viola and backpack take up the backseat.

They pull away. K waves at the other stagiaires who come from towns and cities from across her home state. K feels they are going very fast on the narrow stone streets in the manual car. Each time Armel shifts gears the car moves forward and back. K is not used to this. Armel seems to be reading her mind and begins talking about the Indianapolis 500. She says she agrees, here in France people drive much faster, like they are racing. It is like a race down a very small road.

Armel laughs. No, actually he was saying the family will go to a race this weekend. The one that lasts twenty-four hours. She must be familiar with it because it is very well-known. It is like the Indianapolis 500 but with different cars.

They reach the house. It is large and modern with huge windows in assorted shapes – squares, triangles, ovals. It is built into the side of an earthen mound on top of a cliff. They enter via stairs in the middle of the garage, which is below the house. Once inside, K sees that below them is a narrow green field with a vegetable garden and a chicken shed. Then there is the cliff edge. Then the sea. The tide is in. The lights in the clifftop houses wink in succession.

She kisses each family member twice on the cheek and is told by the mother to relax and sit on the couch. This is your house now and we are your family. Before her departure, K had received some information from the Program, some photographs of the family, the house and the sea. She already knows their names and ages, what they like doing or what they do for work. Gwenn, aged eight, adores animals and bicycling. Rozenn, aged sixteen, plays the pipes as part of a bagad, a Breton band of traditional instruments. M, aged twenty-one, works in agriculture and landscaping. Armel, aged forty-four, manufacturing. Jacqueline, aged forty-three, is a nurse. Their dog Nedeleg jumps into her lap. The cat must be hiding. K can't remember its name.

The family ask about her trip, the flight, the coach ride. She is able to respond to these questions and they praise her French. They offer her something to drink. They tell her she can mix one of these brightly coloured liquids with the water from the pitcher on the table. Gwenn shows her how to do it and is amazed that K has never seen this sort of drink before.

We also have Coke, Jacqueline says, you will of course know that drink, as an American.

No, thank you, K says, I want to try this new drink.

They all sit down around the table where there are crisps and nuts in small bowls. They are talking to each other about their days and sometimes stop to explain things to her, to make sure she understands. Jacqueline says she must be very tired and that they will eat dinner now. She says K shouldn't worry about going to bed when she feels sleepy. The journey was long. And it was her first one, correct?

They eat several courses of fresh seafood. It is delicious though K is not sure what some of the fish and shellfish are called, even in English. She has never even seen them before, and she finds a creaking way to say so, which makes everyone laugh. The family soak up the sauces from their plates with hunks of bread. They ask her if she likes the food and she says she does. They tell her that she will have to make them a pizza like she makes in her father's restaurant. K says she will try but she needs a hot oven. The French word for oven rolls out half-baked.

Next they have cheeses and yogurts. They show her how to add a little ultra-fine sugar to her natural yogurt after she makes a face upon her first bite. Then Jacqueline suggests she might want to shower before dessert. It's been a long trip. M will take your bags upstairs, and Rozenn and Gwenn will show you your room.

K's room has a desk, a bed and a chair by the window, which looks out onto the sea. M explains the electric shutters. When K asks, Rozenn tells her that this pillow is called a traversin. It looks like a hotdog covered in polka dots. The three of them seem to enjoy finding out which everyday things are strange to her.

K recognises the siblings from the photograph sent by the Program of her new family with names and ages written on the back. The brother and two sisters are at the edge of the sea. They have emerged from the water or are about to go in. The rocks curve around them like a pair of hands, presenting the scene to K, the viewer. Gwenn, the youngest, wrapped in a towel, posing for the camera, her head cocked, her right hand encircling her ear as if listening to a message from the sea. Rozenn in profile, long-legged with a T-shirt over her bathing suit, head down, holding a stone in her hand and studying the sand as she nudges it with her toes. At the centre, between them, M stands squarely, his feet planted, his arms loose. He is shirtless, hard-bodied, short-bearded. He stares straight into the lens. At K.

K had committed this image, received months ago along with the Program forms and Pillars and Codes, to memory. She kept it on her bedside table in Indiana. Now this image and its characters are animated for her, in this room, in this house with its cut-out windows that frame all their actions. Squares, ovals, triangles.

Now, M is here. He is living and breathing and laughing at K's uncertainty about everything. He looks her straight in the eye, like in the photo, as if to reassure her he means no harm.

The photograph's subjects leave K to take a shower.

She opens the bathroom closet and examines the small bottles of spray deodorants, shower gels, colognes and shampoos. She doesn't recognise the names of certain scents and tries to work them out by smelling them, by breathing in the scents to breath out new words. She places her oversized bottle of American All-in-One shampoo on the shelf. It's large enough to last six months not six weeks. She places her soap on the floor of the shower stall. There is no soap dish. She places her giant roll-on deodorant in the trash can and covers it up with tissues.

She notes that the shower head is attached to a soft pipe, not directly to the wall like back home. She likes how easy it is to rinse the shampoo from her long hair. She takes a short shower like her mother told her to. Her mother said that when she was in France in the seventies many bathrooms were still outside. People didn't always have showers or running hot water, even then. They heated water on the stove instead. She said they were frugal, the French, and that it had to do with the war on their soil, which we as Americans can't really understand. She said we were never invaded. We didn't have rations. We've had creature comforts for generations, but the French, the Europeans, have not.

K pulls on the loose grey T-shirt that she always sleeps in and some jeans. She doesn't put on a bra because it's bedtime. Her wet hair darkens the lettering of her favourite quotation from a famous, though troubled, male writer. She'd had the T-shirt custom-printed in the shop that does the staff T-shirts for her father's pizza restaurants.

K knows she shouldn't have something covered in so much English. It's probably against the Language Pillar, which says that they are not to bring music, books or other materials in English. She also knows that none of the teachers will see her before bed in her new family's home, so she has taken this risk. As she descends the stairs to the dining room, she wonders if the family will ask her to translate these English words. She doesn't know the capitalised nouns in French, though she thinks she would gather their meaning if she read them in a novel or poem.

She wonders whether she could summarise the sentiment of the phrase, the philosophy it expresses, with the words she has.

> *This is the Great Knowing, this is the Awakening, this is Voidness – So shut up, live, travel, adventure, bless and dont be sorry...*

She is a blank page, but she is also the books she will read, the food she will eat, the love she will make. That is who she is to herself.

None of it is decided.

On her first morning in Saint-Brieuc, K wakes up very late. She has taken full advantage of the electric shutters which thoroughly occlude any sense of planetary motion, of time passing.

When K puts on her glasses and opens the shutters, she can't see the sea. The tide is all the way out. In the foreground of the window frame, a woman rides a dark horse on the beach and puts it through complex dressage footwork. K dresses and goes downstairs, skipping a shower. She doesn't want to appear greedy.

All the adults and Rozenn have left the house for Saturday shopping or appointments. Only Gwenn, aged eight, is home. She is wearing dinosaur pyjamas and watching cartoons. She jumps up and offers K cereal and pain au chocolat, which K accepts. Before K has finished eating, Gwenn says they will now take a little walk to the sea. Gwenn wears rubber boots over her pyjamas and carries a pail, a net and some plastic shovels. K has chosen her waterproof sandals.

They descend the cliff to the beach. K looks back up at the stone steps cut into the edge of the land. There are children everywhere squatting or kneeling in the sand and muck. Craggy outcrops darkened with old and new water lines lean over them. They prod tidepools with their plastic equipment and hold up small fish, molluscs, shells and things K can't identify. Plant, animal, what else is there, K can't recall. The children squint at these findings before placing them back into the pool. The only adult K can see is the woman on horseback in the distance.

Even though the sea is not visible, K is nervous about the tide coming in. She doesn't know how to say this in a way that makes sense. She doesn't know the word for tide, so she would have to explain the sea being far away and then the sea coming closer. She doesn't know the word for drown, so she would have to say killing or dying and that it is the sea, the water, that would make that happen to them.

She wonders if this is the point in the story where one of the children gets badly hurt and she feels guilty about it for the rest of her life and the parents, her new French ones, and the parents of the child who is hurt, think all Americans are bad as a result. She wonders if she is in fact responsible for all these children, or if she is responsible for only Gwenn, or if she is one of the children and someone else is responsible for her. It feels more like Gwenn is responsible for her in this instance. K decides to say nothing.

Gwenn introduces K to each group. This is our stagiaire. She is learning French here and is American. She doesn't know about tide pools. You must show her what is in there. The children take turns explaining the pools and how they work, how there is an incredible number of creatures in each one, and that it's important not to put your hands or feet in them, especially if you are wearing sunscreen. Sunscreen is damaging to the environment necessary to sustain life in a tide pool. Instead, you must lift the little animal with your net or shovel and then put it back very very carefully.

And you must keep the creature close to the pool where it was found and always return it to the same one. Do not shock it by carrying it great distances and leaving it with strangers.

The sea changes every day. She knew about the sky, but nothing of the sea.

K and Rozenn are lounging on the hot patio tiles in bikini tops and cut-off shorts. Rozenn says this is the best. Taking the sun here, not down on the rough beach in the shade of the cliff. The beach is wet and full of salade, algae, anyway, she says. Salade and rocks and little armies of critters digging their way up through the sand.

K is getting brown all over. M will be home soon, and he might talk to them or do some work in the yard below. He might shout up a joke K doesn't understand. He might ask K again if she likes *Baywatch* and Pamela Anderson or Kevin Costner and *Dances with Wolves*. He might explain again that the French destroyed the Bretons like the whites destroyed the original people of America and that is why we are speaking French, not Breton. He might ask his siblings, which now include her, in a baby-talk voice whether mommy has brought kouign-amann from the bakery for tomorrow.

Maybe he will ask K to swim. But maybe he won't because the tide is too low.

He won't smile. He never smiles with his mouth.

His dirty white car charges up the drive. K can hear him get out. Rozenn and K sit up. K blocks the sun with a flattened hand like Rozenn does. M marches up the unfinished concrete stairs. His jeans and shirt are covered in dried mud. He's even more tanned than yesterday. As he approaches no one says anything.

K lies back and opens her book over her face, letting it rest there like a shield. M steps over her into the house and says *Baywatch* has come to Saint-Brieuc. He slides the door closed.

*

K is used to horses, to mucking out stalls and checking fields for holes that can snap delicate legs. She thinks of this knowledge she has brought from back home as she and M approach the green field with its vegetable garden and chicken shed. They have come to gather two heads of lettuce and some eggs for dinner. K is barefoot in the rows of lettuce. The soil is soft between her toes, and she sinks a little with each step. M cuts the heads away with a knife and hands them to her. An iron symbol hangs around his neck on a leather strap. An ornately tooled silver ring encircles his middle finger.

K's hair is wet from swimming. His has already dried. They step through the opening. The dust they've disturbed somersaults in a shard of sunlight.

She wants to kiss him in the musty chicken shed. She wants to cry out that on this very spot there was a flash of lightning and no thunder or rain ever came.

He asks her what they grow in Indiana. Is it wheat.

Sometimes, she says, but more so corn, and little peas, beans, for turning into paste and energy.

He gives her the word.

And in Indiana and Michigan we have tomatoes like you wouldn't believe. They are round and tasty like a big red ass. She blushes and laughs. Her reaching for words has led her here somehow.

Are they juicy he asks.

Yes, very. And with a little bit of salt, they are just right. Salt in a wound she says you know the phrase. She laughs again. He doesn't know it. It's not the same.

Here, we skip the salt. It is always a finger, or a turned knife.

He gives her the word engulf. What the sea does to the shore. What she does to him.

The tide is almost in. Will M ask me to swim in the sea like before. Will he ask me to pick lettuce or gather eggs like before. Maybe he won't ask me to do anything. Maybe he will work on building the balcony steps like before. Maybe he will be in the garage and I won't know what he's doing. Maybe like before I will have to go downstairs and find him so he can say something, so something, anything, can happen. Maybe he won't come home from work right away. Maybe he will have a pastis in the bar down the road and if I wanted to do anything with him I would have to go down there and hang around. I would have to be a person who thinks that sort of thing through. I would have to look down at what I am wearing and decide what it means then decide what it means to walk there. What am I wearing. No.

I would have to change what I'm wearing and walk down to the bar past the old men playing pétanque. But why would I do that. His mother sent me to ask him home for dinner. That wouldn't happen here. He would come home when he was ready. She wouldn't ask or send a messenger. I couldn't say your mother sent me, can you go get something at the store. That wouldn't happen. The store is closed at this time. And anyway his mother Jacqueline would just go herself or have gone already by now. There's no reason to bother anyone about anything in Saint-Brieuc. Pas de dérangement. Everything flows. Ça coule.

There's no reason for me to walk to the bar unless it is to say it then and there in front of the men there drinking.

M will we swim in the bay will we pick lettuce will we gather eggs will you show me how to help you build the stairs.

But then it would be known.

None of these things need to be done more than M needs to do what he's doing if what he's doing is sitting in the bar drinking pastis with the men, and if what I'm doing is sitting in my bedroom at my desk writing poems in French about wasps and danger. I use the English-French dictionary. I look up wasp. Now I can't use it again for a week. I put it back in the drawer. Madame Tanner said to bring one dictionary and that it was to be the only text with English in it.

Use it only in emergencies. Try to say what you want to say using the words you already know. Describe what you want to say with these words. Doing this will make you stronger. We let you bring the dictionary as a precaution. Try not to use it. If you do, wait seven days before you use it again. Instead of the dictionary you must use the words you have to get the words you need.

I could go to the bar and say I need a word. I need a word for an animal that bites that stings that is yellow and black and dangerous. Not a snake. An animal that can make your chest tight if it gets you. The animal flies and is not as beautiful or as important to the world as the one that is similar.

I could put on the new turquoise tank top I bought in the centre of town with the faded purple jeans I got in the vintage store and the brown leather sandals I brought from home that aren't so bad. I could walk in and say excuse me M sorry to bother you no one is home can you help me with one thing.

I just need one word.

The men will say oh it's her homework she's in school she's from America. Why not use a dictionary?

The bar is today's dictionary, one man might say.

No it's for a poem.

Really?

A poet no less?

> *Ô temps! suspends ton vol, et vous, heures propices!*
> *Suspendez votre cours:*
> *Laissez-nous savourer les rapides délices*
> *Des plus beaux de nos jours!*

M, do you remember that from school? Lamartine.

One of the men will say this but M didn't study. That means he and I are different. And this shouldn't be made evident so soon.

There is no reason for me to change clothes and go to the bar to try to make something happen.

So instead I go downstairs for the third time, for the third peach since I began the wasp poem. A kind of reward for another line written. Rapide délice. They are tastier than the overgrown peaches back home. They are round and soft and red-pink like my shoulders.

I think of the word incisor as I pierce the skin. Incisor,

then the shock of flesh and juice in my mouth. I am allowed to say two of three of those words out loud. Flesh and juice. But incisor is out of bounds. What is the word for incisor. I want to say it.

Jacqueline comes in while I'm incising, home early with woven net bags full of shopping from the market. Breads and bottles and a bouquet of flowers.

K, you love the peaches. You must tell me when you like something. I will get more for you.

Yes, I like them very much. What is this, this tooth here?

I put my finger in my mouth and lift my lip.

*

What makes you think you can capture this period in one's life. This period that determines your abiding angle on existence – angle of incidence, or angle of attack.

How will the light off the sea strike you. Will warm air lift you.

Will you be open or closed. Will you be nostalgic or angry or sensual or controlling. Will you be simply alive, or undeniably alive.

Some grown-ups go out to dinner in expensive, overpressed clothes with sweaters tied around their shoulders. Others work as they must while their bodies break down ingloriously. Regardless, most forget the rituals and relics of love and youth.

You will still wear holy medals and triskeles.

You will still bless yourself at ancient wells.

You will still treat certain photographs like relics.

*

Four of them, everyone but Jacqueline and Gwenn, are going to a car race. K has been with the family in Saint-Brieuc for a week. They are going to camp and the race will last twenty-four hours. It is very famous, this race. She is still slow to understand what they are saying, which is a shock because the interview had gone so well. It's clear her French just isn't that good. It is what one calls classroom French. The family are patient with her and repeat themselves using different words until she understands. M and Rozenn and Armel are taking her to the famous car race. K's teachers are impressed by this excursion. It will be a real experience.

When she gets home from classes, she helps pack up the car, an old Volvo which will pull the camper. She listens to them chatting during the long drive. She can't follow very much. M is getting animated about something and Armel is grunting. Rozenn's voice rises a few times. K doesn't think they are arguing, but she's not sure. At one point it seems like they are discussing whether to go to the 'something party something' first instead of the racetrack. She asks them for the phrase they keep repeating, its meaning. Fun fair.

The family arrive at the campground. They park the camper against a chain-link fence. On the other side of the fence is another barrier, high thick metal slats topped with barbed wire. Through the angled slats is the racetrack. The cars are racing by at that very moment. The race has been going for about six hours, Armel says. The cars will be in our ears all night.

It's marvellous, Rozenn says.

The first thing they do is eat. Some men Armel's age join them. His friends from the surrounding area, Rozenn says, they are also camping here. K and M and Rozenn crowd around the little table in the camper and the older men sit outside and rest their plates on a wooden crate. They are all drinking pastis except for Rozenn who is drinking a 1664 beer and K who is drinking a Coke because she not supposed to drink alcohol. They have potato chips with the drinks and then Armel presents the food. It's something fleshy on a real seashell that looks like the one Venus steps out of in the painting. The flesh is golden and bubbly. Armel has cooked it in a little electric camper oven. Now this is very important, he says. This is your first Coquille St Jacques. We say Krogen Sant-Jakez in Breton.

K eats one and then another, thinking these comprise the meal, but soon there are sausages called merguez with rice and butter and some cheese and cured meats too. Then Armel makes coffee for everyone and there is kouign-amann, the Breton dessert they had the night she arrived, that M always wants Jacqueline to buy.

Rozenn, K and M head off to circle the track and watch the cars from various vantage points. When it starts to get dark, they head to the fun fair. Rozenn and K drink Coke and M continues with beer. They buy tear-off tickets and line up for the rides. Rozenn doesn't like the high, fast, spinning ones, so M and K are paired up. One of the rides throws them far up in the air and holds them upside down for sixty seconds. Then it spins them around and around, sometimes very slowly, sometimes at great speed. K feels like she's going to die. They get in line to ride again. This time, once they are upside down and screaming, M unfurls a black and white scarf and hands one end to K so that it hangs between them like a banner. He shouts Bevet Breizh and Vive la Bretagne. The ride starts spinning again. The people below are cheering.

Rozenn is getting tired and says she will go back to the caravan. She tells K to come into the camper later and slide into the bed, don't worry about disturbing her. M and Armel are sleeping in tents outside. M and K ride all the rides again. He explains the scarf and why everyone cheered when he yelled Long Live Brittany in Breton and French.

As they were screaming K had noticed M is missing most of his front teeth. He never smiles with his mouth. Soon there are no lines just people jostling for food and beer and rides. It is two in the morning. K buys a Le Mans 24 hat and a matching one for Rozenn as a gift. M buys a T-shirt. They return to the campground. K gets her overnight bag from inside the caravan and uses the light of the racetrack to remove her contacts. M removes all his clothes except for some black briefs and unzips the tent.

He looks at her now as he once looked down the camera lens. Feet planted, arms loose, shirtless, hard-bodied, short-bearded. He says tomorrow will be consecrated to the race.

K. The photograph. The plans she has made.

*

Her body is not yet fully realised. It is a work-in-progress, like her way with words.

I wonder if you've had a love like this, even once. If there was a love you had one day long ago, a love that you tell stories about. Do you have the words to write it.

*

K has told her classmates they can speak to her mother in Indiana after lunch. K explains that her mother will be awake and always answers the phone. She has permission from Roger, the most relaxed teacher. He remembers meeting K's mother by the departure gates in Indianapolis and speaking French with her. Roger is satisfied the Language Commitment Pillar will be upheld if such calls were to occur.

K was allowed to make an announcement at the start of the morning session saying that anyone who wanted to talk to someone from back in Indiana in French should meet at the phone booth after eating. They would need to use their remaining break time instead of going shopping in the centre of town or whatever they normally do.

K wondered if anyone would want to talk to her mother. She tried to convey with her eyes that her mother wouldn't judge their French and that it would be quite comforting to talk to her, no pressure. If she had said this directly, the teachers might have retracted their permission for the call. They want K's mother to judge the students' French.

In the morning, there is conversation class and grammar class, and both require a lot of talking, which makes the stagiaires tired. They are pushing themselves, and they are being witnessed doing so. In class they are seated at desks arranged in a horseshoe shape around a whiteboard. When they are with their host families they hope something of what they hear of daily life and its expression and intimacy is going in and will eventually come out during their lessons. They yearn to articulate their deepest selves in beautiful singular expressions. During the classes and on breaks, they want to be themselves and make friends. It is unclear on what basis. With all parties at a loss for words, all conversation, even about shared tastes or interests, is not deep or subtle enough for them to accurately differentiate themselves from one another.

On a more fundamental level, they don't want to seem like they can't handle themselves when they leave school to return to their host families. They don't want to be like Rebecca who clearly has no idea what is going on and mostly looks like she is about to burst into tears. When K tries to check in with her, Rebecca can't begin to answer with what's on her mind. If they were to speak in English, they might be sent home or at least given a warning.

And none of them, not even poor Rebecca, want the other stagiaires to think they are undeserving of their place here. Not when So and So from back home in Indianapolis or Fort Wayne or West Lafayette who has way better French should have been chosen instead, how the hell did she get through the interview with Madame Tanner anyway.

None of this is said, but it's behind everyone's eyes.

There is much behind the eyes. The stagiaires couldn't be sarcastic if they wanted to. At their current level, they can't be sly. They are only ever amongst themselves and without teachers at lunch hour. This is when they eat three mysterious courses of food. They must practice eating in the continental style. They fail miserably and end up doing the American pick-up-put-down knife and fork moves again, which are beginning to seem strange after watching their new families deftly create perfect bites – the ideal combination of a bit of this, a bit of that, then a bit of sauce. The knife wielded like a conductor's baton as the fork eloquently conveys the requisite expression.

The stagiaires are only able to be completely earnest and then hope for the best. They can't really speak about their host families beyond their names, ages and occupations, where the house is, what was eaten the night before. They can't talk about their real families in detail either.

If anything else is attempted, anything subtle or comical or suggestive, the others tend to think the person speaking is speaking just to use some words. Many of them do this quite regularly. They talk about things that aren't important, just to use words.

K wonders if they were picked for just this reason, if in the interview Madame Tanner could spot people who would talk about nothing just for the sake of it. Who would use words without putting anything in motion.

How ridiculous it would be to try to explain the sound of M's car tearing up the road when I'm lying on hot tiles in my bikini wondering how I look, and whether he can make me out from such a distance while hoping that when he arrives he suggests we do something. What words could I use to explain the way it makes me feel. It would be only the simple language of liking, which is also loving and nervousness, and the step by step of what happened.

Bikinis, the patio tiles, M driving up and stepping out in earth-stained clothes after a day's hard work and my feelings corralled by the words I have.

Back in Indiana there is no twentysomething guy who looks like M pulling up the driveway. No one like M, who seeing me in my bikini, steps over me and says *Baywatch* has arrived in Saint-Brieuc. Never smiling so I don't know if he is laughing at me for not being Pamela Anderson or if he actually thinks *Baywatch* in Saint-Brieuc is me, which can't be so.

I don't know what he thinks. I don't say anything about it at lunch, even just to use some words.

The summer siblings, Rozenn, Gwenn, K and M, have taken the narrow path down to the water for a swim before dinner.

K hangs back to take it in, the scene from the photograph the Program sent her.

The rocks part to make space at the bottom of the cliff. Their house is up top. Her window with the electric shutters is open and faces the other side of the bay. Her bed has its purple and pink polka dot duvet and long pillow roll. Some notes toward a poem are on her desk hidden under the grammar book. Jacqueline is cooking simple omelettes for dinner, so no rush. The tide is in completely and the water is soft. M warns her that when she steps in it will be up to her neck very quickly so be ready. She thanks him. Rozenn is wearing a long shirt over her bathing suit and wooden clog sandals which she kicks off onto the path. Her shirt comes off and she's wearing a black one-piece. She slides into the water. Gwenn is in boy's bathing trunks and a little tank top. She jumps in just like that. M is already shirtless. She has seen this before at the race track, when he's been working in the garden, and in the photograph. The excess energy running through his frame has gone into making these solid muscles under his skin. He is brown all over. He probably takes his shirt off when he is at work. He is wearing black sweatpants made of soft flowing material. They come down and off and he's in swim briefs. He takes off his triskele necklace with the leather strap and puts it in a pocket before rolling up his clothes and placing them on a rock. He straightens and looks back at her.

Are you coming in? You better hurry up.

K doesn't want to step in and ruin it.

The unveiling of all the mysteries. *Mystères religieux ou naturels, mort, naissance, avenir, passé, cosmogonie, néant.*

*

I have stepped in to present these images and sensations. Have I ruined it.

It’s not really about learning French is it.

This writing began in that incredibly hot summer. The one we just had. The world was ending on all fronts, and it seemed important to locate significant people, significant plot lines.

I was eating peaches and sitting at a desk with my old books. Rimbaud. Duras.

When the world comes down to an old dark wood for our four shocked eyes and a beach for two faithful children, I will find you.

I sit at another desk. And then another.

*

By their second week of classes, the stagiaires are all very tired. Living entirely in another language has made some of them listless, resigned to never fully expressing themselves or understanding anyone else. In the attempt to recreate themselves with the few words they have, they have begun to lose some residual sense of self. The teachers know this is happening but never directly address it. Instead, the stagiaires must engage in role-play during conversation class. This teaches them more of the vocabulary they need to better interact with their families and each other. But it is also draining because the teachers encourage them to act their scenes with the appropriate emotions. This, they say, will ensure that the stagiaires are using an accurate tone when they speak. French is not a tonal language like Chinese, but there are tonal elements to certain phrases in certain contexts. It is not incorrect not to use these tones, but it can certainly help a person integrate more rapidly into French culture if they understand and use them regularly.

Before they had left the USA, there was a reception in Indianapolis with parents and the stagiaires who were to go to Spain, Germany and France. The Program used two cities in France, Saint-Brieuc and Brest. Amy, another student from K's high school, was going to Brest. They were the top French students at their school, and they both had parents who had passports and had been abroad before. The Program always aimed to separate students from the same high school. They wanted to avoid cliques and give students a fresh experience. Some of the larger top-shelf schools had more than two students going, so naturally there might be two to four of them in a given city, but K and Amy were to be separated.

At the reception, the future stagiaires were encouraged to speak English to include their parents and get to know each other before entering this other world to become another self – the one that arises when one lives in another language. All the students were dressed up, the boys in khaki pants and button-down shirts, the girls in summer dresses with cardigans. They all looked the same. Their clothes all having come from the same four stores and been recombined to create similar looks.

There is champagne for the adults and orange juice and sparking grape juice for the future stagiaires. There are finger foods and desserts from the various countries, their origins signalled by flags glued to toothpicks and placed into canapes and cakes. Tea and coffee are served in cups with saucers. The parents mingle along the edges of the room. The future stagiaires try to find others who are going to their city, their country.

The director of the Program, Madame Tanner, is there. She interviewed all the students along with her deputies. She is French but has roots in Germany. Her soft brown hair is pulled into an adroitly coiffed loose bun. She wears classic jewellery with a dress cut close to her figure, its hem just below the knee, and a cardigan draped, not tied, over her shoulders. She is in her seventies. She steps forward and clinks her teacup with a tiny teaspoon. It's a different teacup from the catering set, flowered china in lieu of white porcelain. The room falls silent. She says welcome in four languages and that she would like to say a few words, in English.

Madame Tanner says that the parents have much to be proud of, that these students in this room represent the very best of the state's intellectual achievement and that regardless of the experience they are to embark on, every single student in this room will go on to be lawyers, doctors, scientists, politicians, and will make a mark nationally and internationally no matter what field they choose to pursue. The parents in the room should congratulate themselves on raising their children to be able to reach these heights. These are the kind of students, after all, who do not struggle in school, who understand hard work and what it takes to be successful in every subject, not just the ones they enjoy. These students are also leaders. They are self-motivated. They do not need to be told what to do, they will find out what needs to be done and then determine the best way to do it. These students are also empathetic. They all have shown through various means, whether volunteering or tutoring other students at their own schools or less fortunate schools, that they wish to share their success with others and make the word a better place. These students possess all these qualities, which is why they have been chosen for this Program. Now, I must tell you something that may come as a shock to you, both parents and students. I must tell you that we are sending these students, these future pillars of their own communities, to live under the Pillars of the Program. As a result, they will be diminished. They will for the first time in their lives be diminished, and this is essential, you see.

Madame Tanner translates this final sentence from English into three other languages.

By this second week, they are already diminished – all equally mediocre. There is no real separation in ability, confidence or competency here, and they are not used to this. The shades of difference among them do not relate to their use of the French language or their demeanour in a classroom. Their differences arise instead from things about themselves that they cannot express to each other or to anyone, certainly not with the language they have – deeper preferences and fears, the frameworks by which they live, which are both derived from and exist in contrast to the frameworks of living in their 'real' families back home.

These unexpressed features of the self now loom overly large in their consciousnesses. Suddenly their whole raison d'être becomes the central focus of their meditations, partially because daydreams have become a significant part of their day. They must put the world on pause to rest their ears and mouths. Sometimes they do this in the middle of a class, sometimes in the middle of a conversation with their peers or 'families'. They cannot always be on the look-out for meaning, sorting familiar words and new words into their respective bins and then recombining them to try to make sense of what is being said or what is written. They cannot talk forever around a subject, describing a feeling, action or relationship in thousands of words when one would suffice – if only they knew it. If no teacher or 'family' member is around to teach them the word, they struggle on until their interlocutor grasps where their meanderings are headed. Simple stories about themselves, about who they are, or rather were, can take hours. They only have short breaks for coffees and juice and the lunch hour. When new things happen, it is slightly easier because those things happened in French and it is likely the words surrounding those activities have already been spoken or heard and therefore absorbed. But then there is the question of what kind of person talks about the minutiae of day-to-day life and do they want to be that person, the one who rolls through every mundane activity they have engaged in over the weekend or the night before.

What sort of person gets excited about simple things like gathering lettuce and eggs in the evening or warming themselves on hot tiles like a dog. It's easy to say you went swimming last night, just the two of you, you and your 'brother'. That the others weren't home until later because there was an event at your little 'sister's' school. It is easy to say that you swam for hours until sunset and only returned to the house when it was dark and that your 'mother' seemed shocked because your 'brother' was supposed to prepare dinner. But maybe your 'mother' really wasn't shocked, maybe she thought this would happen. And you could easily say that you and the 'brother' made French fries in the oven and ate them with mayonnaise and ketchup still wearing your bathing suits with towels wrapped around your waists. Your hair smelled like the sea and your toe accidentally brushed his under the table, just for a second.

It is easy to say these things with the words you have gathered so far, even on this, the eighth day of classes when you are so diminished, but it would be much harder to explain what this means in reality. To convey the ambivalence of this scenario, the fact of his age versus yours, of how he looks when stripped down to his swimming briefs, of how conscious you have become of your body in a way that you have not felt before, not even with the teenagers you have been with back home. Does your body seem to him to be that of a teenager, a diminutive adult with, how would you say it, 'baby fat' in unusual places.

Or do you appear to him as a woman, a very very young woman from another country, with long hair and small breasts and curvy hips. The subtlety of explaining that you wonder if he finds your speech awkward or intriguing. Do your deeper preferences, the books of nineteenth-century French poetry that you have brought, seem pretentious or interesting. And how do the answers to these two questions intersect with what the word 'interesting' means in the framework by which you live, or hope to live, versus the framework by which he lives, or you assume he lives.

And is there a shared framework underwater where he disappeared for what seemed like centuries, a shared framework for living found deep in the sea where he dived down beneath you and grabbed your ankles and pulled you downward and still further down until you screamed and struggled. A shared framework, the shock of a jellyfish, no, a squid stunning you and pulling you by the ankles toward its mouth.

Your 'brother' emerges from the water directly in front of you, facing you, quite close but not touching you. He laughs with his mouth closed. He asks if you thought he was dead, killed by a monster. He asks you what you are afraid of.

She wonders how she got so lucky. The other stagiaires would want this. The everydayness of living in pleasure with the one person who gives you nothing but.

K is at Rozenn's bagpipe lesson at the local community centre. She was sent along because Jacqueline said it is a good cultural experience to witness a Breton person getting in touch with their Bretonness. The class is held in a bleak grey room with shabby chairs and a graffiti-covered pressed board table. The lights are off, maybe to save on funds. There are no music stands, so each person's music is spread across the table. The sound is loud and tuneless. Each piper, some old, some young, practices separately and waits for the teacher to come around to give feedback.

K is disappointed to be here instead of at home on the tiles waiting for M to return and propose they do something, or not. The tutor, Gwenael, is young and handsome with hair that is partially shaved, partially mohawked, partially long and partially in a braid. He has a long feather earring in one ear and is wearing boots and a ragged sweater even though it's summer. K wants to kiss him. She imagines what it would be like to hold his hand and be his girlfriend if she was older and more into Breton culture and had fewer stupid clothes and some interesting jewellery.

Gwenael's instrument case has a sticker on it that depicts all the Celtic regions of Europe with their corresponding flags and the phrase I AM BRETON AND PROUD OF IT written in French and Breton. Gwenael speaks Breton and plays various instruments at all the Festoù Noz in the region. Rozenn and M have said they will bring K to one soon and also to a Celtic music festival where they will camp for two nights.

Rozenn is playing the pipes, but with no bags. She has

to get the piping right before she advances to filling the bag and using its power to make sound rather than relying on her lungs. Some of the people in the room have the bags on and are ploughing through things pretty quickly, getting them right and approved by Gwenael and moving on to the next skill. Gwenael goes round and round the square of desks, giving each person some private time. Rozenn's got some tuning difficulties, which K knows because she plays viola. K can read the music even though it's in treble clef because violists are forced to learn it for the high bits even though they read alto clef most of the time. K wants Gwenael to be with Rozenn. K tries to help her do well when he comes around. Rozenn has long legs and long hair and uses good-smelling rose shower cream and perfumes and is fun. She loves Breton culture. She never wants to speak about France or French culture. Never, never French, she told K when she brought out the scrapbook the Program had instructed her to make in order to have something to talk about with her host family.

The scrapbook has photos of K's Indiana family, house and dog and information about her parents' occupations and what she likes to study and do in her spare time. K also created a page on French culture with a French flag and cut-out heads of some French authors taken from an old encyclopaedia set her mother got at a garage sale for her and her brother to use in art projects. K pasted the heads of Victor Hugo and Alexandre Dumas and the cover of *Le Rouge et le Noir* and then wrote some other names – Rimbaud, Verlaine, Baudelaire in various colours and underlined them in contrasting colours as if to say these are the ones she really likes. She didn't note down Djuna Barnes and Anaïs Nin because she thought that might get confusing if they aren't famous enough to average French people, or if they are known for writing sexy bisexual books in English, which are set in France, maybe that's a bit much for an introductory scrapbook.

K didn't put Gertrude Stein down because she hasn't read enough by her yet, and she didn't add Hemingway because though she thinks he is a good writer, he is not her type of writer, and she hadn't wanted her host family to think that she wants to be like Hemingway when she really wants to be like the others. She also pasted in some little cut outs of baguettes and croissants and wine bottles dancing around the Eiffel Tower and the Statue of Liberty, which she subtly overlapped to suggest that France and America are linked. Although she had really wanted to leave America off the page entirely.

When she saw the scrapbook, Rozenn said, no way, I don't do French culture. I only read or talk about it because I'm forced to in school. M agreed and said he felt the same. Gwenn was stuffing baguette crusts covered in Nutella into her mouth as fast as she could until suddenly she yelled with her mouth full of bread, yes, I agree.

Jacqueline intervened. Stop stop little children it's fine she is here to learn French after all and we are speaking French right now aren't we and I seem to remember Rimbaud was quite an interesting poet, absinthe and travel, and I think only seventeen when he wrote amazing works and K aren't you turning seventeen in a few weeks.

K was thrilled that Jacqueline, a nurse, knows these facts about Rimbaud which just proved her whole point that

French (Breton) people are so much more cultured and interested in literature than Americans. Then everything was less tense because Rozenn and M started talking about taking her to a Breton rock concert with the famous Tri Yann, who were playing somewhere nearby on K's birthday. That got M going on Tri Yann, which he explained meant three Johns because of the band members' names and how they sing important songs about Breton freedom from French tyranny, and he said he would make K a tape for her Walkman that night and he did. It became her first and only tape because she hadn't been allowed to bring English music.

All this and the sheer noise of the pipes in the room make K think that Rozenn and Gwenael should be together. K wants to retreat into the little café corner of her head, where she can work on reading her bisexual French poets in French while sipping absinthe like Leonardo di Caprio in *Total Eclipse*. Yes, teenage Leo from *Romeo and Juliet* fucking a nearly bald older man in the ass (who is playing Verlaine). Rimbaud and Verlaine's skins are pasty because they are in London in the winter, and they are very poor and angry all the time with the way society is and therefore must write the most revolutionary poetry the French language has ever seen.

In response to M's *Baywatch* has come to Saint-Brieuc comment K and Rozenn plan a little joke for when he gets home. They are in Rozenn's room in their bras and panties putting together outfits. All Rozenn's clothes are spread out on the bed. K doesn't have anything to contribute because her blocky American clothes aren't appropriate to the task.

Rozenn tells K that they must choose the tightest, shortest dresses they can possibly find. They must look like serious sluts. She says, some of these are from when I was thirteen. They will be perfect and way way short for us now that we have grown.

They slip on the stretchy dresses. Gwenn has come into the room to watch. Rozenn has put on a flowered one. From the back, Rozenn's long legs can be seen all the way up to her ass. K tells Rozenn it is perfect and that her own mother would throw her out of the house if she were to wear something like that. K's peach-coloured dress isn't quite as short because she's not as tall as Rozenn, but the contrast between her hips and waist is made really clear. Rozenn tells her she has a cute shape. Rozenn has a pair of high heels on. There aren't any extras so K puts on her Doc Marten boots with some tall rainbow socks. They each begin stuffing socks into the built-in shelves for their breasts.

No, no! Rozenn says. Let's use these.

She returns from the toilet room with four rolls of toilet paper. They stick them in. They are perfect.

When M sees them in their get-up he laughs and is embarrassed. They demand he take photos of them for posterity. For K's archive, Rozenn says. One day she will be like Arthur Rimbaud and it will all be important, even this. K takes out the toilet rolls and smooths the dress. She folds over the socks so they sit just above the tops of the boots. She actually likes the dress with the boots. Rozenn says she should wear it to a nightclub. Maybe they will go to one before the summer ends.

Nightclubs are sad places, Rozenn says, full of women past their prime and young ones who are trying to get into trouble. The last time M went to one it didn't go so well. Do you know the story of his teeth and why they are missing? We prefer a Fest Noz. But since the nightclub is on the forbidden list, we must go. We will.

K and M are sitting on his bed. He is playing his cassettes of Breton music for her. The door is open and Gwenn keeps popping in to remind them it's time to go down to the sea for a swim.

K asks what happened to his teeth.

M says there are two stories. He told his parents he was carrying firewood up the unfinished stairs at the back when he fell and knocked them out. In reality, he threw the wood and rolled down the stairs screaming to create the full effect. His teeth were already gone.

They laugh at this. K says she can't believe he could pull this off. He explains that only Gwenn was awake and she didn't notice that there wasn't any fresh blood in his mouth. They wouldn't have been able to find the teeth in the gravel anyway. He will get them fixed eventually.

The truth was he had been at a bar and someone, an English person, had said some bad things about Brittany, claiming that the language is brutish, the music is silly, and the people are the least intelligent in all of France. The conversation degraded from there. M came home late at night missing his teeth. The next morning was a Saturday, he did the wood throwing and the family believed it. The dentist will have to put caps on them.

M says that the funny thing is that this English person couldn't speak French properly. M calls him a Rosbif.

It is the Saturday morning market in Saint-Brieuc. They walk together as a family. It is clear that it isn't normal for them to go to the market together like this and that this experience has transpired only because K is here. She thinks it was likely a recommendation in the booklet the Program gave Jacqueline and Armel. This means other stagiaires may be there with their families. There are stalls with seafood, vegetables and flowers. There are jarred preserves and honey and jewellery and scarves. There are framed paintings of sea scenes and women in Breton headdresses. There are faïence booths and Jacqueline explains their significance. K takes some photos of the clever arrangements of goods and produce. M suggests they go to a café for a drink. When they sit down he hands her a little paper package of pink and white striped paper.

Here, he says, from all of us. She opens it up. It's a little silver triskele charm from one of the jewellery stalls. He says the triskele is a Breton symbol of the four elements, earth, water, wind, fire. Jacqueline says that was very sneaky my little M. She asks how he managed to buy it with no one noticing. Armel says K is a real Bretonne now and they are glad she is here. M and Armel have a pastis. Rozenn and Gwenn have a Coke. K orders a little coffee to be like Jacqueline. Jacqueline is having a cigarette and has on her black sunglasses. She is wearing a white linen dress. She leans back in her chair and closes her eyes, saying she is going to catch some sun. K has never seen a nurse who smokes unless it's on a desperate break outside a hospital. She has never seen a nurse who dresses so glamorously on a Saturday and drinks tiny coffees.

The family have stopped at a bar in a nearby town on their way back from lunch. There is Irish music playing. Breton flags adorn the bar and there are signs in Breton and Gaelic nailed to the walls. K sits down next to Rozenn and M in the glassed-in patio. The parents have gone inside with Gwenn who wants to play a board game. M tells K she is having Guinness. She must.

One of the Program rules concerns alcohol. Because it is legal to drink in France at sixteen, the stagiaires' parents had to sign something saying yes or no to alcohol. Even if it is a yes, the stagiaires aren't to go to bars unless with their 'parents' and they aren't ever to go to a discotheque. Drinking is strictly to accompany meals as a gastronomic experience, or, if one is at a bar with the family, a single drink is permitted. K's parents had put an X in the No In All Circumstances box.

M says K must. He returns with three pints of Guinness, which they sip after a toast in French. Then they teach her Yec'hed mat, the toast in Breton. K is wearing her vintage purple jeans, a black T-shirt and her not-too-American sandals. She has rolled up a scarf patterned with tiny pearl and black flowers and wound it around her wrist like a decorative bandage. She has earrings in and her hair down. She feels she has already begun to look better than when she arrived.

K says the Guinness is nice. M is pleased and so is Rozenn. K asks them why Guinness, why this Irish drink for her first alcoholic beverage in France. She doesn't say ever. Why not wine.

Because you are in Brittany they say, a Celtic nation.

And plus, chouchen is too dangerous.

They are on an excursion to St Malo. The families have all made picnic lunches for their stagiaires. Some are in the guise of elaborate dishes in glassware with rubber lids, some are sandwiches bought that morning from the bakery. K has a tin of tuna and rice salad, a small jar of country pâté, a fresh baguette and a pot of natural yogurt. She eats the baguette on the bus.

When they arrive in the town it is raining. The ramparts are dark with water. It is a free day, a self-guided excursion of a medieval coastal town. They must explore on their own and return to the bus by a set time. They are given sheets with all the information on the main sights. No one wants to get off the bus even though they are prepared with raincoats, umbrellas, practical shoes and extra socks for later, just as the information sheet had requested. In their families they've been exotic and interesting. In their classes they've been comrades in their most vulnerable inexpressive moments. Now they are idiotic Americans with cameras around their necks, brightly coloured waterproof jackets and packed lunches, and they must walk the streets of a famous ancient town speaking only French, seeking out sites of historical significance as the townspeople go about their days.

K leaves the rest of her lunch on the bus. She has a cold. She wants to get a hot meal, see the sea and find a bookshop. Steph and Audra agree to climb the ramparts with her. K's nose is running and won't stop. No Kleenex and not a pharmacy in sight. What would M think if he saw her now.

K sees an unattended ice cream stand at the edge of a café's array of tables and wicker seats. On the counter is a metal box of thin napkins stamped with the café's name. She tells Audra and Steph to hang on. She grabs some napkins and wipes her nose. She instantly feels better about herself and this trip. She takes a couple more napkins for later. She asks Audra to hold her umbrella so she can zip them into her coat.

A woman rushes out from the café into the rain. You must not steal, you must not steal. You are poorly raised, she says.

But I'm ill Madame and have nothing for my nose, K says, tears bubbling up.

The woman's lithe body curves over the ugly selfish American like a raised eyebrow.

Here then just take two. That is enough. The woman peels them from the dispenser and hands them to K like they are hundred-dollar bills.

Steph and Audra look on. They say let's go.

The two sheets disintegrate in K's wet hands. Her nose is streaming again.

K gets some words together. You are not nice Madame. You are not a nice woman and this is not a nice welcome to your city. I worry for your business. Goodbye.

K returns from the excursion very ill. She didn't mind or couldn't mind letting it show. She had dragged herself off the coach and onto the local bus back to the house without saying much to anyone. Her friends said they hoped she felt better. The teachers said not to come to classes tomorrow. When she came through the door Jacqueline said to go to bed and that she would come up and check on her soon. Everyone was sitting down to dinner. K was home later than usual because of the trip. She had missed the early evening, her favourite time, the sun, the sea, the garden, the gathering of lettuces and eggs. She concentrated on getting to the stairs and didn't catch a glimpse of anyone's face. She had a roll of toilet paper in her right hand that a teacher had given her for her nose. She let her backpack fall to the ground at the bottom of the stairs and thought about the remains of her lunch still inside it along with the books she had bought. Kerouac's *Sur la route* and *Les Fleurs du Mal*. She remembered when she had arrived with her giant suitcase and they had all laughed as M struggled to carry it up to her room. They couldn't believe a suitcase could be that big and that heavy. A suitcase like this only in America, Armel, her new father, had said.

Before K left, her real mother had said she felt better knowing that Jacqueline is a nurse. Jacqueline came up to check on her. Jacqueline took her temperature and scrutinized the box of American cold medicine K was about to take. K just wanted to sleep and she did.

Hours later everyone entered. Armel closed the electronic shutters. The whole family piled onto the end of her bed. Rozenn cooed that they were worried about her. M presented her with a bottle of Volvic as if it were a bouquet of roses.

Her fever has broken and she needs the bathroom. She wants to go back to sleep and tries to hold it for a bit longer. The electric shutters are closed and the moonlight is locked out. K doesn't usually use them at night so she can see the sea every morning. On her first night, she had closed them at Jacqueline's suggestion that she might profit from a full night's sleep after traveling. From the start K understood Jacqueline easily because she spoke clearly.

When K wrote down the phrases from that conversation in her notebook, she thought about how profit is usually associated with labor in America while in France it was coming up in everyday parlance about rest. Profiting from one's own wellbeing instead of from work done by ourselves or others.

K turns on the light and slides down the hallway to the toilet, which is across the hall from M's room. Afterward she goes to the shower room to wash her hands because there's no sink in the toilet room. All these rooms for different functions.

Someone grabs her upper arm. A hand goes over her mouth. It's M.

Tomorrow you have no school? He slides his hand from her lips to her chin. He keeps the other on her arm. She is not afraid.

Right. No school because I'm sick.

Then tomorrow we go to Benoît's farm to see his poussins. You will like them. Don't tell Jacqueline. I will pick you up at two o'clock and bring you back. Then I will come home like normal and you are in bed. And Jacqueline comes home and never knows. You understand?

Her nose is still running a bit. She hopes it isn't running onto his hand. She doesn't mention it. She says she understands. They are in the dark making plans.

Plans that are along certain lines.

Lines of poetry she has read. You will go everywhere. You have come from always. *Arrivée de toujours, qui t'en iras partout.*

M has invited her on a walk. It is another invitation after the poussins. Rozenn has gone to town to do some shopping with Jacqueline. Gwenn is at a friend's house, Armel is at work. K and M are alone together in the house. She is in her room reading Rimbaud's *Une Saison en enfer* at her desk. He picks up the book and ask her if she wants to walk to the Tour de Cesson.

K can't tell if he's been assigned to take her on a cultural excursion or if this is a genuine invitation. She agrees to go. M doesn't change from his work clothes, which aren't that dirty today, his jeans just stained lightly on the knees. K puts on tennis shoes and sunscreen.

The sun is blasting the bay. They follow the streets through the neighbourhood, past the bar where the men are playing pétanque. M waves to them and they wave back. Words are exchanged and K doesn't catch them. They leave the men behind and keep walking. There are a few people outside their houses fixing things or sitting in chairs in the sun. Dogs bark as K and M pass by. They reach the edge of the neighbourhood and the start of the woods. He stops at the foot of the path. He says, I want you to have walked here in the footsteps of Jean IV, Duc de Bretagne. The man who built the tower. The tower is only visible from down below, from the port, but here we are anyway in his presence.

They enter the woods and walk in deep. The trees are heavy with heat and no birds are singing. They wade through bushes and weeds. She is wearing cut-offs and wonders if there is anything like poison ivy here. They are both sweating. M through the back of his shirt and K in the front between her breasts. Her hair is down and sticking to the backs of her upper arms. They continue until they reach a contorted chain-link fence and signs forbidding entry.

K pokes her hand through the holes in the fence and says she can climb it, no problem.

He hangs back and explains that the tower is on abandoned land. There are unexploded bombs from the Germans who hid there during the Second World War. You step on one and done.

They stand in the heat under the trees. There are some beer bottles strewn around and evidence of past campfires. K isn't sure what to say so she thanks him for bringing her there. She wonders if it's because it's secluded. But surely this sort of place is more suspicious if they were to be caught with its patchwork of scorched earth and litter suggestive of illegality. She doesn't know for sure that he wants her, or what he wants from this.

They hold hands as they walk back down the hill through the woods. They reach the port. The moored boats buzz with voices and flies. Men are cleaning fish. They say good evening to each person in close enough proximity to make eye contact. K feels okay about holding hands because none of the other stagiaires live in this area. She has already asked. The only way she might meet someone is if their family happened to bring them here on a Tuesday evening. It's a working port, not a tourist attraction. She has never seen the teachers down here, or anywhere outside the classroom. They live in their own apartments in the centre of town. They are doctoral students at Indiana University and already speak perfect French. They don't need supplementary cultural experiences.

K and M are holding hands along the port like it's normal. They have a beer at a bar. K is not supposed to do this either. He doesn't tease her about the rules like he and Rozenn did when she had the Guinness. He orders two drafts of 1664. He doesn't say anything about holding her hand or taking her on this walk. Instead he talks about Anne de Bretagne and the meaning of the white ermine on the Breton flag. He says he will lend her a book about the World Wars in Brittany and how in the first one all the Breton men were sent to the front, to the most dangerous spots. They couldn't speak French and the French used them like flesh for the cannon. He says this makes him angry. He doesn't look angry. He looks like he's having a good time.

I reach for his hand and he takes mine. *La promesse d'un amour multiple et complexe.*

I never called you anything. To me, you were a verb. Maybe this is another reason why we could never truly write letters.

So we have this.

*

When he was around her age now, K's grandfather, her mother's father, joined up to fight in the Second World War. He became an Air Force bombardier. He later went to college on the GI bill and became an engineer and beer drinker who never quite got over his time in a POW camp. Her other grandfather, the Italian American one, spent most of his life waiting to fall ill and die. His father from Puglia had died young, following an accident which led to an apparent brain haemorrhage that led to a coma and eventual death from starvation. Her Italian American grandfather was certain he would die early much like his father. Each year he focused more of his energy on worrying about death and every aspect of his bodily functions. He read his own gut like Tiresias reading entrails, which K had learned about in English class.

Last Fourth of July she and her Italian American grandfather had posed for a serious photograph. She had been wearing the American flag shorts outfit her mom had given her two years before. When she was thirteen it had billowed around her scrawny hips and limbs. At fifteen it fit, but its message didn't. Now she was too old to wear matching sets unless they were meant to be provocative in some way like the Santa lingerie sets sold at JC Penney at Christmastime. But this set wasn't that at all and it didn't make any sense on her now. That year her hair was to her shoulders, the prior year's uneven bob having grown out. Her braces had been removed and her teeth were cleaned to a reflective white. She now had contact lenses. She was well into the summer's tan which came up easily for her. She looked worthy of a photograph of a girl blossoming into her beauty, were it not for the shorts set.

Her mother had asked that she wear it for the party. It was expensive. Let's get one more year out of it before we hand it down to your cousins.

Her aunt wanted a photo of her and her grandfather. Everyone was playing volleyball in the backyard while her father barbequed. He had rewired the speakers so the music reached outside. Jackson Browne was singing about The Pretender. Her grandfather was sitting inside on her father's Lay-Z-Boy drinking vodka with tonic. K had been sent inside to check on how he was doing. He had a sweater on. It was ninety degrees outside.

He said it looks like they are all having fun and that he was so proud.

Her aunt came inside after her. She knew her aunt wanted a photo of them because she thought it might be his last summer even though the doctors had detected nothing. His colour was bad. He was thin. K looked down at her American flag set. She moved to stand next to her grandfather who remained seated in the Lay-Z-Boy.

She says let's do a serious one. She stands upright and places her hand stiffly on his forearm as it rests on the plush chair. Her fingertips graze his bony wrist.

He says ok, let's do it. She knows he isn't smiling. She isn't either. Her aunt laughs and says you both look so serious. Like you've just arrived at Ellis Island or something.

On the Fourth of July in the Breton house on the cliff, it is decided that they will watch *Dances with Wolves* after dinner. It is an American film Jacqueline says, you can't get more American than Indian. They all drape themselves over pillows and across the floor, couch and armchair. Nedeleg the dog sits on K's lap. Gwenn laughs and says Nedeleg prefers K to everyone else. K doesn't sit with M as it seems too obvious. They may or may not have heard them these past few nights. K thinks she would like to one day sit next to him on a couch and have it out in the open.

She feels she has been opened up, explored. It has only been his hands and tongue, the same as with others who came before him, but it is enough. It is more than enough for K. She is holding the thing back because it doesn't seem necessary.

They watch as Kevin Costner, the soldier, starts exploring the West on his own only to end up fighting and fleeing his fellow soldiers. They watch the territories and people get opened up and wounded. They watch the people dying. At the end the family wishes her a happy Fourth of July and ask what it is like to celebrate Fourth of July in America.

She says it is a bit of this and a bit of that, the Fourth of July.

*

When they reach their tent, they pull each other down to the grass. They unzip it and enter on their hands and knees. They take off their clothes and toss them into the corners with the blankets. She pushes him backward until he is flat on the plastic floor. She removes the scarf from her wrist and ties it around his eyes. All his fingers have disappeared. He is laughing.

She has read about this somewhere in a book and yes, it is wonderful. He smiles, open-mouthed, his missing teeth forgotten.

She tells him to tear her apart.

What else is there other than the simplicity of ecstasy. Why do anything else. Why proceed further. Why go beyond these images.

Why not insert a car crash or flood or political unrest for contrast. No, leave it.

*

But the saints aren't real. It is idolatry. Christ has redeemed us. The Word of God is all we need. Élisabeth, or Elizabeth as she was formerly known, says. A small group of stagiaires are walking through town to the Monoprix after lunch. The others are clearly uncomfortable. K thinks the statement is in reference to her holy medals which sometimes pop out from beneath her shirt. She has three, two of which were given to her at a family party before she left. There was a sheet cake decorated with the Eiffel Tower and the tricolour and Bon Voyage K. About forty people, including aunts, uncles and cousins on both sides, were gathered. K's grandmother gave her St Christopher, patron saint of travellers. Her Uncle Vito, her godfather, gave her St Catherine, patron saint of Paris. They had been blessed by the parish priest Father Michael. Vito also gave her a vial of oil that had touched the glove of Padre Pio. Keep this with you, he said, and bless yourself with it. He is not a saint yet, but he will be, and he's even from our region in Italy.

Uncle Vito explained Padre Pio's stigmata. He had had quite a lot of wine and began weeping at the corners of his eyes when he described it. The men of the family were sitting around the dining table drinking wine from small tumblers instead of the crystal stemware K's mother had put out. K knew at an early age that once the wine was poured into the tumblers there would be the agony and the ecstasy. The important things would be put on the table – politics, religion, food – and these things would be gone over intently, opened up like the belly of a fish readied for cooking and eating. There would be lightning flashes and softer gentler moments when the men wept. If any women were in the room, they would look relieved at this show of emotion, as if something they knew was true had come to pass again.

K tried to stay at the table for the duration of this ritual, though most of the women and girl cousins drifted to the kitchen to wash dishes while the boy cousins shuffled around purposefully, pretending to clear the tables and take out the trash then diverting to the garage to spike their Pepsis with whiskey.

K's going-away party had featured one of those gentle moments of hushed voices and admissions of ecstatic connection with God and food, with the family's God of food, bread, oil and bitter herbs, of holy bodies and blood and water and relics. With the Padre Pio oil, Uncle Vito gave K two large cans of special tomatoes and a small tin of very good olive oil .

K already knew about stigmata from the *X-Files*, but didn't say so. She wanted to hear Uncle Vito speak of it.

K wants to have stigmata that smells like roses. She especially wants these stigmata to appear suddenly while she is walking with Élisabeth. She wants the power of God to flow out of her body in floral-scented blood. Who wouldn't?

Élisabeth is missing the point about the saints. They are always getting torn up, tied down, achieving the unachievable. Their bodies are incorruptible, eternal. K thinks this is beautiful and has nothing to do with shame, with sin. The saints are naked with hard bodies and intense stares.

K has a tiny blue and silver Virgin Mary that was given to her upon her first communion, the size of a pinkie fingernail. The two new medals she was given are heavy and depict the saints' heads and bodies in 3D. They are more obvious when she wears certain shirts. She doesn't wear a scapular, like some of her cousins back home.

Élisabeth is talking about sin now. Pécher. Which is also to fish, pécher. The sound is the same. I sin, je pèche, sounds the same as I fish – je pêche – and I peach. Élisabeth sounds like Élisa-stupid. At the Monoprix I buy a tight white tank top with a built-in bra and spaghetti straps to free my shoulders and silver medals.

I peach.

The beauty of repetitions. Of bread. And wine. And water. And blood. And the body. The infinite white cloth laid out and folded away again.

The star weeps pink in the heart of your ear.

Dark blood on your flank. The sea going red.

K waits at the gates of the bank with her travellers' cheques and passport. Men in suits come and go via the main entrance. The smaller gate for the bureau de change opens for only one hour a day. This part of the bank is cold, dark, wood-panelled. There aren't many tourists in Saint-Brieuc so there is no line. She changes another hundred dollars earned by working in her family's restaurant. She knows she will go back to Indiana at the end of the summer with no money left. She knows that this summer she will spend every cent she has ever made on the things that matter, books and food and drink and voyages, and that this is what she will do, always. This is how she will live.

There is surely something, not in the Three Pillars but somewhere in the Codes, something prohibiting dating of any sort. It would be too isolating. If we dated a fellow American, we'd be more likely to give in to speaking English and isolate ourselves from the rest of our classmates. If we dated a French person, we wouldn't spend much time with our families and benefit from the full cultural experience. We are meant to be like nuns or monks, cloistered in contemplation of the trinity of grammar, vocabulary and culture in that order.

But what if one of us dated an adult, a member of our family, and what if this is the full cultural experience, what if the grammar and vocabulary of it marked our body, our language, our culture, for the rest of our life.

What if we knew that's what we were doing all along.

The bombs of the past could go off at any time like the ones installed by the Germans at the Tour de Cesson.

Her past is so simple but she has not made it herself. It is formed mainly of grains of hope and the impressions of others. If she's not careful as she traces its sandy edge, she will wipe it away completely.

The line for the phone booth is ten deep. K is inside talking to her mother.

K is proud her mother can do this for the others. She thinks that each morning her mother must be at home in her robe making coffee and wondering if a call will come from France. K is surprised that so many people are homesick enough to speak to a complete stranger in French about what's happening in Saint-Brieuc and what they miss about America. K is also happy that her mother's interrogations of her experience will have to be cut short.

Her mother is doing her best at pushing K and preserving K. It involves what she wears and who she meets.

In the future, her mother will keep a stack of K's publications in the living room next to her brother's scientific articles. She will house them in a little shrine with dried flowers and a candle and photographs even though neither of them has died.

In the telephone booth K doesn't know any of this will happen. Though she is working on the story in that moment, she doesn't know she will also write it and that her mother will read it, and so know it.

She doesn't know it will exist to be discussed in terms of its style, characters, politics and attitude toward sexuality.

As with any minute detail of her life, she hopes she will write it, that her life will be worth writing about or that her writing will be worthy of the life she is living.

Finally, she hopes that someone will read it.

She tries not to think of her mother reading it, her life.

This pulse of writing life and living a life worth writing is always there. She knows this is naïve. She knows it is a cliché. She knows it living it and she knows it as she writes this, now.

K waves forward the first person in line.

They reach the church as the bells are ringing. K has worn her only dress, red knit. It holds her close and buttons from the V at her collarbone right down to her knees. She wears her brown leather sandals. She had put her hair in a high ponytail and then braided the ponytail tightly. Her flowered scarf is tied around its base. He has on some newer jeans and a soft black button-up shirt. He holds her hand as they walk up the steps. She doesn't know what to think of this. She had asked the family about going to mass on her first day. They'd seemed a bit shocked and then amused. She had been warned by her mother that the French are very secular, that they have the best churches but didn't really use them, and that it is mainly old people who go to mass regularly.

In Indiana she and her family go to mass every Sunday. K is a youth member of the parish council. She sits in the monthly meetings and makes suggestions, some of them quite creative – one was to buy a large glass box for people to slide their private petitions into and let the amount build up as a visible symbol of those prayers that were too personal to be read out at mass. This wasn't taken forward by the council, but the priest, Father Michael, had liked the idea and praised it. He had asked her to join the council after their conversation in the rectory the previous year.

K had phoned the parish office and requested a meeting. The purpose of the meeting was for Father Michael to explain why he didn't address the reading from Paul to the Colossians in his homily the previous Sunday. She told him it was an upsetting passage for women in the church and that he should address it, not just pass over it and focus on the Old Testament and the Gospel. He said he understood and would be sure to talk about it next time, and that he would put it in context as K was asking him to. While they were on the subject, she asked him why women couldn't be priests. She might have liked to be a priest, to do it the way Father Michael does it. They were in the rectory office, which was full of antique furniture and books. The parish secretary had brought them iced tea and closed the door. They were sitting on either side of a round side table that held an intricate antique marble and oak lamp depicting the Virgin and Child.

Father Michael is a young priest. Nearly every evening he plays basketball at the hoop behind the rectory. He wears normal gym clothes. When the youth group had a car wash to benefit Habitat for Humanity, he wore a shirt with the sleeves cut off quite low so you could see his bare chest through the sides. His chest has just the right amount of dark brown hair on it. He helped scrub the cars for charity wearing that shirt.

Father Michael could have been one of her older cousins. He came from one of the other Italian families in town, one of the very big ones. Coming from such a large family means at least one person has to be donated to the church. That, and Father Michael loves a good mass. He puts on a great show. He even reinstituted many of the formal elements of mass just as most churches were removing them in response to pressure from evangelical Protestants given their disdain for pomp. It was thought by most Catholic priests and bishops in the US that the best way to respond to the austerity of Protestantism was to imitate it, to pull back on the flinging of holy water, the wafting of incense, the veneration of saints. Father Michael went in the opposite direction. It all came out, including the optional longer list of saints invoked at the consecration. K had not heard of Linus, Cletus, Clement, Sixtus, Cornelius, Cyprian, Lawrence, Chrysogonus, Cosmas and Damian before.

With Father Michael, the youth group swelled its numbers. One week a husband and wife came with baskets full of holy medals of the Sacred Heart of Jesus for the boys and rings with tiny roses on them for the girls. They handed out little yellow cards with red lettering that said Purity Pledge at the top. The youth were told to think about it while they had their pizza and Pepsi and that if they signed the pledge, they would be given a ring or medal. They could then keep the card in their bibles at home. There was no pressure. They could go home and talk about it with their parents and Father Michael would have the rings and medals on hand. The couple concluded their presentation and invited the kids to have some pizza. K slid the card into her back pocket and joined the line. Some of her older cousins in the youth group were helping with the pizza. They were meant to be mentors, senior kids others could come to with questions. She wondered what they thought of this but didn't ask. She didn't recall them ever wearing rings or medals that meant this. This was something new. She hadn't yet had what the married couple who brought the cards called 'intercourse'. She had done what was called by the teenagers 'everything else'. After the pizza, she and everyone else signed their cards and took the medals and rings.

She quite likes the ring's simplicity. The rose is open and full in contrast to the thin band. It could be a ring that means nothing or anything at all. It could be a ring signalling the opposite of purity, whatever that is. She wears this ring, always. And it could mean many things, including whatever she wants it to mean at a given time, just like the rose itself, the flower.

A rose is a rose is a rose, she read in English class. Gertrude Stein.

The previous three Sundays the family had had other things planned. Last night Jacqueline had said M will take you to mass tomorrow if you like.

K didn't really want to go anymore, but she did want to go on an outing alone with M. They had done what was called 'everything else' but had never gotten dressed up and gone anywhere early in the morning together.

Everyone else is still in bed. He makes her a coffee with milk in a large bowl and holds her waist with one hand while she drinks it standing at the counter.

She imagines the photograph of this scene. She says aren't we a picture, a saying in English. He agrees immediately. K doesn't know whether he knows what she means.

They leave without eating anything. They are nearly late. When they enter the stone church, it is half full and nearly all the heads are silver. There are a few families, but no small children or babies. Some men stand in the aisles at each side and everyone else sits on wicker-bottomed chairs. There are no kneelers like in her church at home. M and K stand at the back for the mass. She feels like she is watching rather than participating. She doesn't say any of the responses, which are in French, so she doesn't know them by heart. She doesn't beat her breast and say my fault or trace a small cross on her forehead, lips and chest when she is meant to. It is cold in the church and it smells musty. There are a few small shrines dotted around with a few candles burning at each one, some with ancient wooden statues painted in faded reds, blues and greens.

When it is time for communion, she goes for it but M does not. She is the youngest woman in the church and she is in a red dress. She wonders if the priest, a short man with white hair, will refuse her. A priest back home might refuse if the person wasn't recognised, if the priest couldn't be sure that they had been confessed. The person would be given a blessing in that case. She faces the priest, he gives her the body and she moves on, stepping aside to cross herself while facing the altar. There is no blood. She returns to M at the back of the church.

He says let's go have a drink. At the bar he doesn't make any comment about the mass or about her wanting to go. Through the bar's glassed-in patio they see the parishioners leaving the church. The bells are ringing again. She wonders if the mass-goers notice that she and M are inside drinking pastis. It is eleven in the morning and they haven't eaten anything. He asks if she wants a sandwich or something. She says no. He orders two more drinks. He puts his hand on her crossed thigh and slips his fingers into a gap between two buttons of her dress. He says he can't believe his luck.

They all go out for lunch in a town forty minutes away. They take two cars. K, Rozenn and M in his car. Armel, Gwenn and Jacqueline in the other. The summer is waning and it is important to Jacqueline and Armel that K has this experience.

K would prefer to control the weekend hours and go off with M in his car, but it would be the height of impoliteness to say so. So she puts on the red dress once again. While M once again wears his black button-down shirt and newish jeans with leather shoes. The rest of the family dress in similarly nonchalant outfits. The lunch is gourmet and it is delicious. Each course is intricately presented and paired with appropriate wine. As one of the wine bottles is decanted, the sommelier holds a candle flame below its neck so it can pass through at the right temperature. They all laugh when he has left the tableside. The family understands these gastronomic practices, knows about them and diligently explains them, but they don't require their implementation to have a good meal. When they finish, K thanks them for an incredible experience.

On the drive back it rains. M smokes out the window. The windows fog up and soon they have to roll them all down. They turn Tri Yann up loud and sing about the prisons of Nantes, each in their own key. Rozenn's long legs are stretched across the back seat.

La fille était jeunette.

Rain has also fallen on Saint-Brieuc, on the Tour de Cesson, on the house on the cliff. M says we should go walk a bit and check on his land, the parcel he just bought near the cliff path to the sea.

No one tries to join them.

They pass through the paved streets of the neighbourhood and onto a dirt road. They enter the fields, the ground is muddy. He pulls her along faster and faster until they are running. It is raining hard now. Steam is rising from the grass. They pass through a grove of small trees and the sea appears at the bottom of his land at the edge of the cliff. His land is a long and narrow green field with nothing on it but a small wooden shed. He takes her inside. There is fresh straw on the ground. He pulls her dress off her shoulders with both hands. Afterwards he smokes a cigarette outside as she gets dressed. It has stopped raining.

I am convinced by all of this, by the land, the sea at the edge of the cliff, the fresh straw on the floor of the shed, his hands in my hair, his efforts with nineteenth-century French poetry, the rose ring's meaning for me, the triskele necklace's meaning for him, the wine we shared in the streets of Lorient like any couple in love. I ask him, formal word choice, if there will be other women after me?

I know there will be other women after me. I ask anyway. I am convinced by all this. I am convinced by his saintly incorruptible body, by us at mass together, by me in this close-fitting red dress and him in his black shirt. I am convinced whether we are standing together in the back of a medieval church or here in this field. I want him to know that I have never not been convinced, that this was deliberate and wholehearted and not accidental, haphazard or touristic. That I am not an innocent child, a victim, nor am I a sinner in need of a forever from him to be saved. I tell him I have planned all of this from the start.

You know this. I know this.

En route to the bus stop, K finds a flattened cat. It is still alive and breathing. It is lying in a pothole that outlines its shape like a shell around a walnut. It has a tire track along its side. She encircles the pothole with some large rocks and runs home to try to catch Armel, who is always the last to leave in the morning. When she finds Armel she doesn't know the words for pothole or flatten. She repeats the phrase wounded cat again and again. They drive off toward the pothole and he gets out first to examine it. Armel doesn't seem surprised by what he's seen as he returns and restarts the car.

He says she has done the right thing by creating a barricade. He will drive her to class and then come back for the cat.

K thinks about the cat all day at school. She doesn't tell the others about it in case the cat has died. A lot of them are missing their pets at home and they don't need to know this story unless it's accompanied by a happy ending.

When she gets home Rozenn is in the garage peering into a large box. Inside is the cat, slightly less flattened now. They take turns feeding it milk from a little bowl held to the side of its mouth. Rozenn has cat food too and it drags a couple tonguefuls into its mouth. They take some old T-shirts and surround the cat with them like a nest.

K and Rozenn are petting the now unflattened cat. It is still nestled in its box in the garage. It is eating, drinking, pissing and shitting on the shirts, which they must change each day. Rozenn holds a damp warm towel which she uses to steam clean the cat's fur because it can't groom itself. It is purring. K thinks about how a year ago she was poulticing her horse's foot. The horse she had gotten for a song, a horse of her own at last, an ex-racehorse that she was going to train to jump. The horse was injured and must have been sold to her doped by the Michigan stable owner to conceal its ailment. A week after the stable owner sold her the horse, he shot himself. His stables were liquidated to pay his debts.

She had ridden her horse once before the drug wore off and it went lame. Then, over several months K had to give her all sorts of treatments. As a result, the horse could be handled in every which way and never got spooked. By winter's end her horse was back to health or seemed so. K sold her with full disclosure to a family who wanted a trail horse. The same day she loaded all her tack in the family mini-van, drove it home and stored it in her parents' garage.

If the horse had been able to jump, she would have been at all the big shows this summer, not here.

She wants to tell Rozenn this story but it is too complicated. There are too many technical words for the treatments, which K knows Rozenn will be interested in because she loves animals and wants to be a veterinarian.

Rozenn and K rise to go inside for dinner. The cat leaps from the box and runs out of the garage. Rozenn and K run after it. The cat disappears as M drives up. His music is blaring from the car's tape deck. He has brought mussels and bread and cider. There is ice cream and it is melting. They help him bring it in.

The sun is blasting the gravel and the sea is deep blue. The chickens are still pecking at the seed she and Rozenn tossed into the yard. The cat is gone. The horse is cured. She isn't a child anymore.

There is a Fest Noz tomorrow, he says. We will go.

They are lovers. They can't stop themselves from making love. K is at her desk alternately studying grammar for tomorrow's test and writing a poem in French. She has moved on from the playful wasp poem and is trying to create an image of the sheep grazing on the seaweed at low tide juxtaposed with the horrors of the D-Day landing. She is studying Rimbaud's *Le Dormeur du Val*. She is trying to make the images of the sheep and the soldiers interlock with each other, and the whole poem culminate in a final line in which we realise the true cost of war. She is doing this without using the English-French dictionary. She flips through the French dictionary in search of interesting words.

M comes in. He is home from work and his clothes are wet and torn and covered in stains. K can hear cooking noises downstairs and smell potatoes frying. It won't be long. Gwenn is squealing at Nedeleg, who barks. Jacqueline hushes them, laughing.

M closes the door.

He tells me what is going to happen and why. We leave the window open onto the sea and the sun and the rows of lettuce in the garden below. We proceed quietly. We hardly move. It's like it's not happening at all.

It is Rimbaud's poem, the stillness of the soldier, the two holes in his right side, like Christ.

The boats lean on their sides and their anchors grasp the wet sand. It's hard to believe they will hold when the tide returns then float up to right themselves on the water.

They each carry something to help Armel clean his boat. K has a large brush on a pole. The others have buckets and soap and scrub brushes and towels and a special liquid to treat the wood. Armel rolls a cigarette, puts it between his lips and lights it. M is already smoking. Rozenn asks K if she'd like a Coke. Sure. Several families are doing the same, cleaning or making small repairs. The green arms of the bay hug the dark patches of boats and their people.

She thinks of her last visit to her grandparents' lake house before she left. It's not really a house, more of a trailer built onto with clapboard rooms, indoor-outdoor carpet, and a toilet and sink connected to a water and sewage line. Her grandparents, her mother's parents, do stay up there overnight, but not when it is too hot because there is no air conditioning. They weren't there the day before she left when K and her brother drove up to do some fishing. Her father's old flat-bottomed boat was too heavy for them to get into and out of the water from the seawall so they were to fish from the shore. They picked up some bait from the shop just across the Michigan border, a small Styrofoam pot of earthworms and some wax worms as well, which the bass prefer.

Her brother liked to fish for largemouth bass. Catch and release. He liked the struggle of reeling in a strong bass and always brought a tape measure so he could note down their size. K didn't like handling their narrow bodies and their lack of proper scales felt wrong.

She preferred the rounder scaly bluegill that you could grip easily and keep to eat depending on its size, though she hated it when the young ones swallowed the hooks. Sometimes she could get a hook out by carefully peeking down the throat and wiggling it free. Then she would throw the fish back. Sometimes it was clear when the fish landed that it wouldn't make it. It couldn't right itself and swam in curves around the legs of the pier. Her father always said it was fine and that a snapping turtle would get it. It will all be over quick, don't worry. Sometimes the hook went deep into a tiny young one's throat and there was nothing to do but tear it out and feel the metal drag through the heart and ribs. The young ones were so small they weren't worth cleaning. K would set the little fish gently into the water, say a little prayer and watch the blood encircle it.

Each summer she and her brother accumulated as many bluegills as they could and then their father or grandmother cleaned and froze them. At the end of the summer, they had a fish fry with sweetcorn and sliced fresh tomatoes with onion, vinegar, salt and pepper. Both sets of grandparents would be there and the grown-ups would drink mixed drinks first and then beer and wine. Some years the haul was meagre and their father did Alaskan king crab legs as well. The day before she left, she and her brother had brought in a good amount of bluegill, their biggest haul of the summer and possibly ever considering they were only fishing for a couple hours. On the way home, there was a thunderstorm while the giant sprinklers out in the soybean and cornfields were still running. The surges of white water looked like clouds against the black sky.

Once they got home she had asked her father if they could just gut and clean the fish, fry and eat them that night because she would be away for the whole summer. Her father said no, that it's tradition to wait until the very end and there was barely enough. Now she wonders if her brother is catching any bluegill without her and if the freezer is getting full. She wonders if they will wait for her to return to have the end of summer meal.

When they finish cleaning Armel's boat they are all tired and hungry. M says he felt like he was at work and that next time they should bring another strong man, one of his friends, to help with things. Benoît would be happy to come, for example. Armel doesn't reply.

They stop at a crêperie on the way home. K tries brut and doux cider for the first time and has a crêpe with cheese and mushrooms inside. For dessert she has one with butter and sugar. The others have eggs in their savoury crêpes. They all feel better now and have slight sunburns that enhance the effect of the cider. M asks the owner if there is any chouchen. There isn't. M promises K she will have some before she leaves Brittany. She must have some.

Jacqueline says, Be careful with our K, M, she is precious and she doesn't belong to us after all.

One of the teachers, Sophie, is French. She is from Strasbourg and brings up her vowels from deep inside her body. On lunch breaks she smokes and drinks black coffee outside the canteen. K told her on the first day of classes that her mother had studied in Strasbourg in the seventies. Sophie said that must have been interesting. K thinks Sophie believes the rules are too strict yet she is the toughest in implementing them. She is the only one who has given the stagiaires a glimpse at her life by bringing a small suitcase to class on Fridays before she gets the train to visit her boyfriend. She teaches the culture class, which focuses on French history as well as artistic and social elements, including the continental eating style some of the stagiaires are close to mastering.

The cultural workbook has reproduced cartoons from newspapers and other sources to depict aspects of French life and politics. One of them is a yellow hand with black lettering 'Touche pas à mon pote!'. The previous week the stagiaires had been assigned a conversation with their families about this hand and its meaning and were told to report back their learnings in class the next day.

Later that night K had shown it to M and asked him what it meant. They were naked in her bed and the moonlight wasn't enough to see by. M turned on the small lamp on the bedside table. He sat up to study the page. K stayed under the covers. He told her the image is against racism. He said that pote means friend, and that actually it comes from a Breton word paotr. He closed the book and turned out the light.

The next day in the culture class it was clear K hadn't

had the kind of detailed conversation that she was meant to. Other stagiaires reported that their families had explained immigration to France from former colonies and negative attitudes toward the new arrivals, which is what this hand was trying to address. A few families were not pleased with the hand's message as they thought that French and Breton cultures were the ones to be protected, to not be touched. K said that pote is derived from a Breton word, so perhaps it's more complicated than that.

K looks around the room at the faces, all white, except for Ramona, whose father is Native American. This is not how her school looks back in Indiana. The students here have been chosen from the best schools in the wealthiest areas, or, like her, plucked from among the rest. All their trips have been paid for by their parents. The stagiaires are, Madame Tanner had said, the best of Indiana. This cannot be true.

Today they are meant to be having a conversation about what they will do at the Fête de Familles, which will be held at a local community centre three nights before their departure. There will be drinks and snacks, a rendition of *La Marseillaise*, which they are practicing, and a series of little performances and speeches. It is a chance for all the families to come together to celebrate the achievements of the summer. The stagiaires had been instructed to bring a more formal outfit for this, which is why K brought the red dress. She wonders what M and the family will think of *La Marseillaise*, the plans to celebrate France, not Brittany.

The stagiaires who play music or have other talents are

meant to offer something. K plays viola. Sophie knows this because K had hers on the plane. She had told K she would make a note of it.

When Sophie asks her what she will play, K says she would like to recite a poem instead.

Sophie asks if it's one of the poems in the coursebook that she wants to read, *Le Lac* for example.

K says it's not that. It's *L'invitation au voyage* by Baudelaire. K says she bought the book in St Malo.

Sophie mouths the lines:

> *Aimer à loisir,*
> *Aimer et mourir*
> *Au pays qui te ressemble!*

M asks her what she studies, what she wants to do after high school. She says she will go to university for English and French literature, and she will write poetry. He did not go to university. He did a training course to work in horticulture and landscaping. He knows how to change the gradation of the soil so it drains as it should, how to shift the rays of the sun by turning the land. He knows how to move heaven and earth.

When she says of course I will pleasure you, he explains the word and then how the verb works in this way, how she works for him.

She reads his sex like braille.

They destroy his sheets with red streaks from their hands and bodies. He says not to worry, although it might shock his mother when he does his own laundry.

The triskele symbolises earth, fire and water with air encircling it. His triskele is made of iron and hangs from a brown leather strap. He gives it to her the day she gives him her rose ring.

He puts the ring on his pinkie for a moment and then in a little leather pouch on his bedside table where he collects the coins, fossils and polished glass that the sea releases onto the shore each day.

We must make an exchange, he says. He puts the necklace over her head and pulls her long hair through the loop of leather.

They are talking about the holy spirit on the way to Monoprix. One of them asks another whether she has accepted Jesus Christ as her personal saviour. Yes, that's important. Yes, have you. I'm Catholic. But the pope. The primacy of the word of God. Then why ministers? Why not just sit in a room and read on your own? Jesus was a teacher, a rabbi. We need teachers. No, we don't. We don't need no education. What? Pink Floyd you know. Yes, but you just said about five English words! I'll tell the teachers! Art is its own religion. That is all we need to worry about. Art and the body. That's why Protestant churches are boring. No half-naked Jesus on the cross spurting blood out of his side. No glowing white limbs to imagine your own legs tangled up with. Blasphemy. Not even a thing anymore goddamn it to hell so, whatever. Wow, what does that mean? I can only guess it's something bad in French that you asked your family to teach you. And I thought you were a nice girl. Well I am, are you? Come on guys it's fine, everyone's having a good time. Let's just get to Monoprix.

Their red and white have mingled again. They are lost and have lost any good judgement. She's not sure what language she speaks or what her name should be. She mouths more new words each day. The others always correct her. He never does. He reads Rimbaud's *Ma Bohème* to her when she asks him to. He says he is not a good reader. She tells him he sounds fine to her.

She wonders how she can do it. How can she live the life she's meant to. And what and who is meaning it. What if she stayed and became his woman in this town, in Saint-Brieuc. Would that be better than – what else. This may not, will not, last forever. She has her whole life ahead of her. She will go on to do great things. This is what she is told by everyone.

He is smoking a cigarette by the window. The lights on the ships out at sea tap out an illegible signal. The house feels awake in the heat.

He tosses the cigarette out the window and opens the door to let the breeze pass through. He turns off the light and gets back into bed.

Armel and Jacqueline never make their bed. When their door was open K noticed this.

The poem is coming along. It is unfurling in K's notebook. All the vocabulary is going into it. It is in prose. She is sure it is useless. She is sure there is nothing in it. She knows it is empty. It is only words. She doesn't have feelings for these words yet, she hasn't had feelings in those words. But they are beginning to come together. The words and the feelings are approaching each other. There are things happening and the words surround them, or the words make these things happen in the first place. There are feelings in and around these things and the words brush up against them and sometimes they stop and get to know each other. The words and the feelings speak to each other. They take their time at this. Some words are sitting in her heart. They are resting there for her to use one day, for her to explain all of it deliberately and with utmost precision. These words are the most accurate words to explain this. They are the select few words he says to her when she is lying back and being taken and being given to. They are gorgeous words and nasty words. She is both the best and the worst girl alive. She contains all these words. They flow out from her and he breathes them in and releases them into the air like smoke. He doesn't put the words onto her. He reads them straight off her flesh and she is grateful for this. He is a good reader of all the words that comprise her, her at her most degraded and her at her most regal. Everything in between. He reads words on her that she doesn't even know yet. She must note them down here in this poem. She must find a way to work them into its structure. There must be a way to use them at least once, though they are best when they are repeated again and again, when they chime with each other in exactitude. She is certain she can find a way to work them in because these are the words that are true.

The poem says she is kneeling in the fresh straw. The tiny poussin is in her cupped hands. The two young men are watching her, smiling. They are drinking beer from squat green bottles. She is afraid to breathe, that she will shatter its bones. She is afraid that she will crush this offering he has made.

The friend says it.

I told you she would love this, didn't I. I told you her little heart would break.

It is her birthday. She arrives home after her classes and goes up to her room. Her blue bilingual *Complete Poems of Arthur Rimbaud* is on her bed. It is open, face down. She hadn't left it like that. Underneath the book are two tiny presents wrapped in flowery paper. One feels like a card, so she opens it first. Some of her notebook paper has been torn into rectangle. Written with her purple pen is the phrase, 'Dix-sept ans! Tu seras heureuse! – A. Rimbaud'. Along with the note, a condom. The other box is perfume, Rose Ispahan.

She is transcribing the Breton songs into her notebook, the ones in French. She is playing them back on her Walkman. Young girl, prison, hanging, wife, sailors, workers, peasants, hay, land, chains, madness, mourning, gull, gorse, love, nation. When he returns she will ask him to check her work.

The family drive out to the countryside to dine at a traditional Breton farm. They are seated around an ancient table. They are the only people there. Food is brought in on wooden platters and the cider is in gourd jugs. She notices the staff are not in costume despite the setting. They wear contemporary clothes, unlike the medieval experience outside Chicago where wenches serve ale and overcooked meat on the bone and there is fake jousting and sword fighting. Armel tells them to focus on the different tastes of the cured meats in front of them. They are made from different animals – deer, rabbit, wild boar. The staff explain the range of preparation techniques and parts of the animals that have been used. They say to taste one and then have some cider before you taste another. K tries a dark slice. It tastes like a barnyard. She takes some cider into her mouth and the taste shifts to herbs and salt. She takes another slice and it is different. There are pâtés to try as well. The main courses of rabbit and pheasant come out in large earthenware pots for sharing. The waiter serves them each their helpings. He is the owner and this is his farm. They eat with heavy antique knives and wooden spoons and rough breads for sopping up the liquid. Then there are cheeses and rustic desserts. M says he will take her around the farm. He has done some work here before so he knows it well. The owner says be my guest and bows. The others stay back for coffees.

M leads her along the oak-lined path past the pens where the animals are eating. They enter a building where meats are hanging to cure and then another barn set up as a dining room, like the one they were sitting in.

They choose a table and use it.

Rimbaud says of departures – enough seen, enough known, enough had.

K says never enough.

Leave or stay, there are new sounds and new stations in life. Morning and night.

It is late. They should separate and sleep in their own rooms, but she is losing two nights with him. She is leaving very early in the morning for an overnight excursion to Mont-St-Michel and the beaches of Normandy. Jacqueline will drive her to the coach pick-up at six am. He could stay in her bed but thinks it too risky, that someone will come upstairs and find out. Sometimes he seems very worried they will be caught. Other times he doesn't seem to care. K isn't sure it would matter if they knew, but maybe it would. They aren't like her own parents, but they are parents after all.

He had offered to drive her to the coach but Jacqueline insisted on taking her herself. K wonders if she is wary of what they look like together. There are only so many nights before K leaves, before she's gone from this house on a cliff in Saint-Brieuc. The stagiaires will leave Brittany to spend a week in Paris before they fly home.

It is July. The days are getting shorter now. She wants to say this to him. She wants to say that the corn is knee-high now in Indiana, knee-high by the Fourth of July, as they say. She wants to say her mother is mowing the grass. She is not there to do it. Her brother is at baseball practice running from second to third. At their restaurant, her father is unloading three months' worth of mozzarella with all the young men, but not with her.

She could be there wearing a long white apron tied at the waist. Her hair in a braid down her back, hands on hips as the semi pulls into the parking lot. She can carry a good amount of cheese by herself. The days are getting shorter. The peonies are long gone and the lilies are coming into their own. There is a vase of two strains of lily from the backyard on her bedside table and her books hover around her on shelves. Some are quite rare.

Some boys are calling her and she is going on dates to the movies. Some of the boys are actors and some aren't anything yet. They might drive across the Michigan border to a field and park the car and lie back together under the sun or the moon to see what a body in this world is for. There might be a storm. They might decide to run through puddles under lightning at the edge of a soybean field.

The next morning she will ride a horse and count the strides in between the jumps. Afterwards she will hose the horse down and slide a thin piece of metal along its body to pull the water onto the ground. She will paint its hooves with dark oil and then shave the insides of its ears until they look like pink shells. She will be alone, driving the country roads and thinking, stopping to buy a Coke at a roadside shop.

Thinking of him, of this.

Always the photograph with him in the centre, surrounded by rocks and the sea.

She planned it on the horizon at the end of a furrow in a cornfield just before planting, a field of potential.

She stretched that field across land and sea to reach another green field at the edge of a cliff.

The field where eggs and lettuce are gathered.

A story that is a series of images and sensations remembered and imagined – which makes it a poem.

It is the sea mixed with the sun. It is eternity. It is skin gone brown and the sea gone out. It is the eternity of bread and wine and salt from the sea dried and placed in a finger bowl. It is a fish opened up, its bones slid from the interior with expert hands so you feel safe eating it. It is holy relics in their monstrances. Coils of hair and shards of shin and hip. Teeth. Tokens of love exchanged like rose rings and triskele.

It is found again.

I will go everywhere. I have come from always.

One of the first things she notices about the house is the lack of family photos on the walls. The only wall decorations are the windows themselves, the sea beyond. It is as though Gwenn, Rozenn and M emerged from the sea without history to sit down at the dining table and await their four courses. K's mother would be shocked by this apparent lack of veneration on the part of Jacqueline and Armel. Blown-up photos of K and her brother and family line the walls of their living room. Her mother mounts and frames each image herself. Everyone who visits notices this exhibition, the quality of the photographs and the professionalism of their presentation. There are two of K in her First Holy Communion clothes, one with her great-grandmother from Italy. K wears gloves and a white veil and holds a rosary and a little white book.

There she is at a horse show. The horse's mane is braided and woven into tight knots, which she had accomplished over several hours. She is still learning how to braid the tail properly. There is her brother in a reproduction Revolutionary War uniform. He tried it on when they visited a battlefield. There is K on a rock with the wind blowing through her hair. It is on an island in Lake Superior where they have reintroduced wolves. K and her family had reached the island by ferry last summer, the month after her grandfather died. Everyone on the ferry vomited over the sides. K and her family took some heavy medication and laid themselves down on the benches at the centre of the boat. They slept the whole way there and none of them dreamed of cancer, hospitals or what summers used to be like. They spent two weeks hiking and had a narrow miss with a mother moose. Their boat had drifted toward a moose calf which was eating water plants in the shallows. The mother was about to charge them. K's father got the engine of the boat running just in time. They sped back around the island to the lodge where they ate pork chops with potatoes and apple sauce and Oreo cream pie.

When she had friends over to the house, especially guys she wanted to date, she was quick to move them on from the family exhibition. She didn't want to be the same person. The same person who does whatever it is with a guy on a date and the same person missing her front teeth and holding a brace of blue gill. This archive is not of her making. She has not defined its parameters or its tone. She was not the one who stopped time with the shutter and extracted a fragment of a moment, which is what her mother is always trying to do – extract her life's pleasures and fix them down firmly with a mount, a frame, a wall. K wants to move forward, not back. Some of the guys who come over are fascinated by this evidence that she was always beautiful, talented and loved. K knows this is inaccurate, a stylisation. She knows this even more so now. She stops to snap photos of the scenes that lay before her in Saint-Brieuc. Photos to keep with the first.

M, Rozenn and Gwenn at the lagoon. M on his twenty-second birthday cutting the cake with a giant knife. Her desk with its neat piles of papers and books. Herself in front of the church at Sainte-Mère-Église, unsmiling, the American and French flags heavy with rain. Herself with her backpack on at the airport gate marked Paris-CDG, her medals caught on the zipper of her travellers jacket. The evidence in these photos is like the evidence in the aerogrammes she sends to her mother. It is partial, removed, gathered at least one step back from the scene. In the scenes themselves, she is right there, trying to speak, trying to love, trying to form an archive of the present in her bones and on her tongue.

She wants to read and write poems that speak of lovers drinking each other, swallowing and eating each other, inhaling the other into the body.

You cannot mouth a photo the way you can mouth and breathe words and skin.

You cannot display what has been taken and held by the sea unless you breathe over the waters.

A bed, the land, my hair.

Years on and I have not brought those old photos of us here, to the sea at Ardmore, in Ireland, where I am writing this.

Instead, I breathe in the sea, the words I can remember, and I breathe out this, your skin.

At a certain point the family all know but it is never said. There is no such thing as consequences for your actions here. There are only actions. The path to the sea is there. The sunlight mixing with the sea and warming your face is here. To have eternity, you must take that sunlit path. You must step into the sea.

Jacqueline has said M should take K to Lorient for the special concert on her birthday. She has bought them tickets as a present. It is just K and M who are going. They will camp. That is what is going to happen. They pack the car. They go. They park the car, set up their tent and start walking toward the stade de Polignac. They buy a rustic pizza from a bakery and a bottle of rosé. They find some steps and sit and drink and eat. He holds her thigh. He necks the bottle. She has thanked him for the perfume but they haven't discussed the other package. She has both presents with her.

The stadium is a small local football pitch. The concert is ecstatic. They are right up at the front near the band. The crowd is leaping up and down and singing along. She knows the words to some of the songs from the tape he made her. Now a soft song is played and the singer is speaking. She recognises what he is saying. It is a meditation on Breton identity. It ends with the words 'discovery or ignorance'. She leans in and tells him she has his other package and that yes, she is now seventeen and she will be happy.

We reach the tent. We undress and get very close. We can hear music. We lie on our sides facing each other in a tent in a green field. It is still light enough to see.

*

M takes K and Rozenn to a nightclub. It is strictly forbidden by the Program so he has chosen one out of town. It has an older crowd. There aren't many people his age and there are no people K and Rozenn's age. The doorman seems both surprised and pleased to see them and says their entry is free. Only M has to pay because he is man. Rozenn and K get a free drink each. All they have to do is tell the bartender that the doorman said the young ones get a free drink. Then they can order two small liquors, not beer or cider, but whiskey, vodka or gin in thin plastic cups with two ice cubes. The music is loud and not Breton or Celtic as she's become used to.

K tries a whiskey and Coke. Her older cousins like to make whiskey and Pepsi when they think no one is watching. It is overly sweet but she drinks it anyway.

K and Rozenn take to the floor. She thinks of the parties back home. Some of her friends had the kind of parents who would rent out a whole city park pavilion and hire a DJ for their son or daughter's birthday. She has photos of some of these parties in a little album in her room in Indiana. Everyone, both boys and girls, wears jeans and T-shirts and baggy plaid shirts, which they tie around their waists when they get too hot. K loves dancing at these parties. This surprised her at first. She doesn't love the music or the feeling that people are pairing off, but she loves the sweat, the bodies, the lack of conversation.

Now she wonders how that feeling of abandon was ever possible with parents in the room. She feels embarrassed for herself and vows not to go to these parties again. After the festivals, concerts and bars of this summer what would pavilion parties feel like anyway. The dances in the school gym sponsored by the Honors Society or other school groups to raise money always had themes. The last one was the 1970s, which had been her idea as President of the Honors Society. She had made her own bell bottoms and bought a vintage top and silver shoes. Her mother helped her flat iron her hair. She had fun at this party, but again there were teachers and parents there.

The thought of it makes her feel strange. How could these people spy on them like this? It feels to her that something must be wrong with the adults who want to do this, who want to watch young people being free with each other. She thinks of her and M simply moving through the world together.

She thinks of the phrase you should be ashamed of yourself. She thinks of the phrase shameless. She thinks there is no shame when things are confessed, noted, spoken. In confessing, shame is punctured, toppled, wrecked – if it ever existed in the first place.

Live, travel, adventure, bless and dont be sorry. The T-shirt says.

Shame. I cannot feel it now and did not feel it then. I confess.

At the club Rozenn is wearing a black shirt and a flowing flowery skirt with heeled clogs. K is wearing her red dress again and the brown leather sandals. As soon as she walks through the door of the club she wishes she hadn't. She and Rozenn look so young and like they are going somewhere special, not to a dark nightclub with older people dressed almost entirely in black. K wishes she had worn her purple jeans and black boots. She feels weak and curvy in the red dress. She doesn't match the music. The drink eventually kicks in and she and Rozenn dance. They try to stay away from the men on the floor. There aren't many of them, but they seem unaware that M is watching from the bar and that they are with him. She thinks it shouldn't actually matter whether or not they are with M. She thinks she would like to be left alone with Rozenn to just dance – left alone within a crowd. It shouldn't be so difficult because that's what she thought dancing was about. There are comments from the men on the dancefloor and along the railing that lines it, comments that remind her and Rozenn that they are being watched. The men are under the impression that this is why K and Rozenn are at the nightclub, to be watched.

It's getting late. Rozenn goes to the toilet and K goes to the bar to talk to M. She hasn't seen much of him all night, only when she came to the bar for another drink. He leans against the bar and pulls her hip into him. He asks her if she's enjoyed the night in the club. She says sure, it's been fun to dance. It's always fun to dance. The men in the club are watching her and M. Now they know she is his. M says it's a strange club, it's for old people, really. Look there, he says, look at that vielle salope. K turns toward the dance floor, which has cleared except for a lone woman dressed in a black lace top with a short black skirt and spike-heeled boots. She is dancing. She has black curly hair cut into an angled bob. K knows the first word means old, but she doesn't know the second. She knows that the totality of what he's said isn't kind. She doesn't want him to explain this word, this new piece of vocabulary she is supposed to diligently gather. She watches the woman dance, alone but in a crowd. The woman smiles. The men at the rail yell and gesture at her. K can't make out what they are saying.

She can imagine its meaning.

The bus full of stagiaires reaches Sainte-Mère-Église in Normandy. Each year, the town marked the American sacrifices that led to it being the first to be liberated on D-Day. Outside in the rain in front of the town hall, they met the mayor and sang *La Marseillaise* and the American national anthem. The formal clothes they had been instructed to wear for the ceremony were hidden under brightly coloured rain jackets. Afterwards, each stagiaire was introduced to a townsperson who would host them for the night.

K and a stagiaire named Tracy were hosted by a woman called Marie who lived alone in an ancient house in the centre of town. Her children having grown and departed for other corners of France. She served them pork cooked with prunes and potatoes and various Norman cakes for dessert. Then she presented them with a Sainte-Mère-Église souvenir plate that showed the church and the paratrooper who got stuck there. Waves of paratroopers had drifted in on the wind. Many were shot by the Germans as they floated down or became ensnared by their chutes. The paratrooper on the church survived by playing dead. Now he is remembered with a mannequin in a uniform attached to the church exterior. K and Tracy slept in twin beds covered in lace ruffles. In the small house they resisted whispering into the night.

The next morning at the beaches the tour guide asked for a show of hands from those whose relatives had fought in the Second World War. K raised her hand. I can tell you, he said, you would not be here today were it not for the D-Day landings. K thought of her grandfather, of his basement full of tools and antique guns. He went every Tuesday and Thursday to the American Legion where he talked to fellow veterans and drank beer, her grandmother's life revolving around these two days a week. Nothing could interfere with the Legion afternoons. Her grandfather's family fought in every American war, including both sides of the Civil War. There are framed medals and bullets and bits of uniforms hanging in the living room of their house, as well as five antique guns on a rack above the fireplace. Her grandfather has a spoon with a swastika on it that he keeps in a drawer. It is his soup spoon brought back from the POW camp where he was held. Without D-Day he would have died in that camp. Without D-Day she would not be here.

K knows that her parents met when her mother was fifteen. She knows that in their youth her parents were what was once called wild. They smoked cigarettes and went to concerts by all the major bands of the day. It was the late sixties.

Father Michael tells the youth group that everyone must do their best to treat their sexuality as sacred, to not use it for their own pleasure but instead for the glory of God through marriage and children.

Years later I find Father Michael on social media. He is not Father Michael anymore. He lives in a big city in another state. He writes about that city's socialist history and gives political tours. Michael interprets the relics of the past. I buy his book.

They are sneaking out of the house to swim in the sea at high tide. There is a full moon and it is late. They are raw. He says they must stop or they will hurt themselves. He brings a small flashlight and they run through the neighbourhood laughing. They follow the trail down the cliff to the lagoon. They take everything off and jump in. She has never swum naked before. She can feel salt-water sliding inside her. It must be a good thing. The moon is close. She scrapes her leg on a submerged rock but doesn't mention it. She can't believe they are there in the sea in the moonlight, that they are naked and alive in this world. They haven't died in war or from a disease. They have enough to eat. They have everything. They are everything. Then quite suddenly she feels that they are creatures and that all of this can change. They could be pulled under by the tide going out. There is a catastrophe coming, a catastrophe they can do nothing about. It is too late. They can only wait for it. She is leaving. It is ridiculous for her to think this, but she is alive and so she thinks it. There is nothing else to think in this moment. The sea will be there and the moon and he too. She will not be there. This is a catastrophe. This is the end of the world.

Her wardrobe door is open. She is looking at herself in the long mirror. He is behind her pulling her hair back and up. He eats her neck.

At the Monoprix Steph and K buy tank tops. In France the clothes fit people. In America T-shirts are squares that hang down from the shoulders. Steph and K are sick of this. They long since solved the jeans problem at the weigh and pay vintage shop. French jeans legs are not squares resting on the ground. They are cut close to the thigh and calf. K's purple pair are from the late seventies. K spent nearly all her extra money on a brand-new pair of black Doc Martens boots to go with those jeans. She put royal blue laces in them and they gave her blisters that turned into flaps on her big toes. It looked like the bottom layer of her toes might fall off. Jacqueline checked them. She gave her dressings and told her not to wear the boots until they healed. She said the flaps would fall off and tough skin would emerge. She said the boots were now pressed to the shape of K's feet and her gait, all thanks to this pain she had experienced.

Steph and K want to get more of these shirts that fit them, that hold their bodies and reassure the world and therefore them that they are not dumpy square-shouldered Americans. They share a dressing room. Steph has large breasts. She puts the shirt on and immediately there is this fact. In her square shirts she just looked big from shoulder to waist but in fact she has very big breasts and a very tight belly. Steph's skin is paler than K's. Her host family doesn't live on the sea. She knows about K and M. She is the only one who does.

They both look in the mirror. The shirts are an electric blue. Steph's is a slightly lighter colour and has a deeper V-neck. They both have long dark hair and blue eyes. They have some of the best French in the group. They both read literature because they like to. They had bought novels and poetry on that rainy excursion to St Malo and inscribed their names, the date and the city in the upper righthand corners of the first pages. Even if they hadn't come here to be locked into the Pillars and Codes they would have been friends. K wonders what they will say to each other when they can speak in English. When they will be able to go beyond liking or loving something towards a more refined answer, a discussion of the poètes maudits, for example, or books that aren't in French, like those by Anaïs Nin and Djuna Barnes. K wants to put her hands on Steph's waist and trace upwards to her breasts and test how the shirt fits. K wants her hands on her tight belly.

Steph is an artist and brought sketch pads and charcoals with her on the plane. She has just bought canvases and paints to take back to her house in the centre of town. Her family lives in a large apartment building. Their apartment is over four floors. She has no siblings there. They are all grown up. She is close to the mother, that is why her French is so good. They talk about everything in the morning over big bowls of coffee. The mother smokes and Steph smokes with her. Steph has extra time in the mornings because she lives in the centre of town and doesn't need to get a bus from further out like K and other stagiaires.

Steph says French women are wise and don't put up with nonsense and that she has learned a lot from her mother. She tells K that is the mother's message to her, and therefore to them. Steph is adamant K must listen to this as well. It is very clear. American women are far too soft. The mother says American women behave as if in a dream and so let themselves be wronged. Wrong first if you must. Remember, you are the desired one. Keep that in the forefront of your mind, always. If we must have these eyes all over us when we are simply walking down the street, at least remember this truth before you give in to some bastard. Look after yourself, by yourself.

Steph is the only one who understands the importance of this experience to K. She is the only one who will protect it.

K has told M about Steph. She has said Steph knows about him and understands everything. He says we should meet her sometime, have a drink.

Some of the stagiaires have also made the promise. To guard their purity. Some of the girls have had special dances with their fathers. Some of them say that homosexuals will go to hell and that lust is the enemy. Others are on the pill and it was their mothers who took them to get it. They miss their boyfriends back home. Some don't care about sex and are more worried about the next school year.

K tells them that the key is to be like you are gay no matter who it is. Mouths, hands. Then you don't have to worry about much of anything. She promises them this.

K is practicing her Baudelaire poem for the Fête de Familles. She asks for feedback on her pronunciation. M tells her the poem is sexy and that all the men will surely clap for her. She asks whether the women won't also find the poem sexy. He says the women will see that it's a young woman with her life ahead of her being addressed in the poem and they will be jealous. The women will know that it is in fact K who the poet is speaking to and not them. This is why they won't really clap for her. K says no it will be me speaking the poem in my woman's voice. I could be saying this poem to anyone in the room. I could just as easily be saying it to you as to a woman, to a young woman like me, or to anyone at all. I could address a poem written to you to a woman instead. I could have written this poem. He says this is exactly why he doesn't talk about poetry.

K has gone into the cathedral by herself at during lunch break. She reads on a small plaque that the reliquary contains a piece of the true cross, a thorn from the crown of thorns, the skull of Saint Guillaume and a relic of Saint-Brieuc. These are locked in cases behind an iron gate.

K lights a candle at the foot of the the Madonna. She sits on a wicker-bottomed chair and puts her face in her hands. She prods her eye sockets and chin with her fingers. Culture class is in the afternoon. Today they are talking about the Middle Ages and have read extracts of a poem called *Le Roman de la Rose*. The story is the Lover seeking his Rose. The story is about eternal virginity, which is symbolic of a deeper truth they will examine in their discussion.

The story is a series of images and sensations remembered and imagined, which makes it a poem.

I want it to be so I must stay forever. I want to live on his land in a tiny house and write poetry.

All this must happen without me seeing my real family again.

Perhaps I will have a terrible accident and be hospitalised in a coma. My brainwaves on the screen responding only to his voice until everyone else loses heart and leaves. He stays. He reads me poetry every day and massages my limbs so I don't lose muscle tone. When I wake up, I am fine, but it's clear I must stay. No one argues when I say I must stay forever in Saint-Brieuc. I have just survived a terrible accident and a coma and the person who revived me agrees.

The accident must be reversible. It is merely an instrument to achieve my aim. It is when I have attained what I desire that my thinking becomes dangerous.

This is when the plot of the tale must turn back on itself and there must be retribution for the sorcery I have engaged in. If the story ends with the aim achieved, nothing comes after because the gathering of eggs and lettuce is drained of meaning – the love we make has become quotidien so too the tower and the undetonated bombs. The sea is simply there and the relics in the cathedral turn overfamiliar.

There is no life after attainment because then the memory of this summer and what it has become for me fades. To stay is to destroy the summer and the myth and therefore the self. The self I am now.

I is an other in Saint-Brieuc.

K always thinks about what she was doing a year ago on a given day, two years ago, three, ten, twenty. She is sure this practice dates from that summer, this counting and factoring the distance between beauty and its aftermath. The worry that any given present moment can neither be held nor compared.

Twenty-two years ago today was July 27, 1997. Were we at the music festival.

Or was this a normal school day, or another day of being *Baywatch* babes. Was it a day we all swam together. Did we have fresh fish bought by Armel on his way home. Did M give me the blue shirt from his compulsory service in the French army. The one with the tag sewn inside the bottom hem where he had inked his name, an ermine and BEVET BREIZH, Long Live Brittany.

Was this a day I wrote a poem, plucking words from the French dictionary and scattering them across the page like dice.

Was this the day he showed me his land and said he would never sell it. It was too narrow for a big house so it would always be safe, and he would preserve this piece of the Breton coast forever and the only creature to dwell on it would be a horse for me to ride on the beach when I return.

Was he certain twenty-two years ago today that I would return. Did I accept this certainty or did I change the subject. Did we lie back in the grass on his land and seal it. What was the position of the sun and the moon.

When I return to Saint-Brieuc, three years later on a day in September, M is living around the corner with his girlfriend in her parents' spare house.

On that day, I am twenty and have taken trains to Saint-Brieuc all the way from the Ardennes where the night before I slammed vodka tonics in a bar dedicated to Elvis that opened onto the main square of Charleville, the square where Rimbaud had pranced and smoked how many days and years before I got off the train alone in Saint-Brieuc and M wasn't alone, and he said his land had been sold and the house on the land next to it was torn down and a big house was coming to straddle both parcels, and the horse he had rescued two years before had died while he was trying to bring it back to health. The horse with its ribs showing in the photos he had sent me. The horse he called Hermine, after ermine, Brittany's emblem.

Despite my measuring, my shuffling of dates, my attempts to nail myself to the cross of the hours – which are the hands of the clock that winnow my body, that winnow every body. Despite my intoning of the necessary phrases, I could not pinpoint the moment Rimbaud walked off from Charleville to Paris to follow his letter to Verlaine. I could not dig down into the bottomless mud of the Ardennes to carbon date something, anything, fungible that would have absorbed his traces.

I could not draw that line of red and white and sweat between me and M from that summer into that September when I was no longer seventeen. The archives give no evidence of our exact movements, only a series of impressions and images brought together, and only after the indulgent and indecent struggle buried beneath these pages.

Nonetheless, I have arrived here just in time to create the necessary juxtapositions, a series of images and sensations remembered and imagined.

The words are tasting and drinking and eating and drenching.

They are walking to his field.

Hello lovers! A boy shouts from atop the hill.

A note on her pillow, in English. GOODNIGHT MY GODDESS.

She is supposed to be keeping a journal. This is a suggestion in the Program guide, which means it is more like a requirement. Instead, she sends her mother prepaid aerogrammes in French a few times a week which capture the day-to-day minutiae that would have been collected in a private diary. They are only allowed three such letters in English over the course of the whole summer.

She tells her mother in a mixture of French and English about the baby chickens but not about being sick. She describes the lettuce picking but not the lightning strike. She explains the triskele but not the way it hung around his neck. She says they swim all the time but not that it is in the middle of the night and they are naked. She has the aerogrammes for one life and then she writes poems with words she finds for this, for what is really happening. The new words she finds symbolise still other words. If she can't find the words she actually wants, she must remake the ones she has. As a result the poems are in a kind of unbreakable code. She can never go back to when these words were unknown. She can't trace them back in time to before they came to mean something to her as she was writing them. He doesn't read her poems, doesn't ask to. He sometimes brings her a beer at her desk when he gets home from work if that is where he finds her. He says this will help her write and that she should take her time. He doesn't want to disturb her even though she wants to be disturbed.

She knows the words now, and she has used them. She has studied them at a high level in the context of great literature.

*

A series of deaths. The older ones dying one after the other in a great chain of cancers and heart attacks and unknown or natural causes. The first she could feel was her great-grandmother, dead at ninety-two, born in 1894. She had immigrated from Italy when she was a teenager. In her final years it was as though a swathe of words in her limited English vocabulary vanished each day. Then came the deaths of her children and their spouses, including K's grandfather who died the summer before she went to Saint-Brieuc. K had sat in the hospital hallway and heard him scream in pain after radiation treatment. He called his wife's name over and over again as if she could stop it, as if she could snap her fingers and they would be sitting together at home watching the Cubs lose, yelling at the television, each with a vodka tonic in hand and a couple of grandchildren sprawled on the couches calling the pitches. They would cook pasta with fillet steaks for the kids and the freezer would be stocked with every ice cream bar imaginable.

The older people of the town itself were dying as well. Italian Americans, all known to each other, who passed through the restaurant most mornings for a cup of coffee with her father or grandfather. If it was a Saturday K was often there slicing ham or rolling pizza dough, badly. The old men would come and talk about the newspaper's contents or the Cubs or politics or nothing in particular. If it was summer they would talk about winter weather. If it was winter they would talk about summer weather. They were always looking forward. To baseball season. To Christmas. To one of their children's babies being born or a divorce being final, God bless.

For the run of funerals, K had a special long black dress from Ann Taylor that nipped in at the waist. Her mother helped her set her hair in hot rollers so it would fall down her back in soft curls. Her mother leant her a set of pearls – a necklace, stud earrings and a matching bracelet. Her grandmother leant her a black cashmere cardigan to wear in the chill of the funeral home and told her to slide a Kleenex under the sleeve in case she needed it. They stood in receiving lines for hours and at the close of day they said the rosary with a mixture of Sorrowful and Glorious Mysteries. The older cousins smoked outside and no one said anything about it. These deaths loosened her grip on her own story and how it might end as she became a relation to fewer others. As the deaths continued she knew more and more would come. She knew then that she was stumbling toward her own death. Her limbs would shrivel or she would lose her mind or a sudden cancer would take her before either of these things could happen. That much was certain.

That same year, a student from her high school killed himself. He played second violin in the orchestra. All the orchestra members went to the funeral and sat in the organ loft because the church was so full. The student's mother was by herself in the first pew. She had no one to tell her to hold it together for the children and teenagers who were there. She had lost her only son. He was her only person it seemed. She wept without ceasing throughout the service. She tried to give a speech but it could not be heard or understood and so it could not be remembered. The students never saw the mother again because she never needed to come to a concert again. The mother never again needed to pick her son up from school or have a meeting with a teacher. She no longer had things to do related to having a son. It was like she was fourteen again and had no rules or obligations. She may as well have had a completely different life because the one she had before was cut off, cut dead.

I have not thought of this mother until now. She was probably my current age back then, or close to it.

The recent or impending deaths in my life, in life, must have had something to do with what happened here.

With what is written here.

One of the things listed in the travel insurance document K has in her folder is a confirmation of the complete reimbursement of repatriation costs. Her parents had bought the highest possible insurance coverage as recommended by the Program. This will ensure that if she dies she will be returned to be buried in American soil in the Catholic cemetery in Indiana. She will be buried near her great-grandmother and her grandfather and others on the plot including her grandfather's sister, who died aged five of burns inflicted by a boiling pot of pasta water that was pulled over her when the children were playing wedding in the kitchen. Anna had been the bride. She was draped in lace tablecloths and flour sacks. They had stood Anna on a chair to see her better and she reached for the pot and no one could stop her. All the trailing fabric had held the scalding water close to her body. A scald is deep and penetrating and keeps burning long after its initial contact.

If K died and was repatriated, she would be buried the morning after the Mysteries were said. Whether or not M would be invited is not indicated in the insurance document. What she might die from is unimaginable. This is what insurance is for. It is not to predetermine outcomes or divine the specifics of managing those outcomes. It is to mitigate against sweet risk.

*

She is flushed after two whiskeys with Coke and two ciders. She and Rozenn are dancing a Scottish, a paired dance, in a community centre in the countryside. It is a Fest Noz. Rozenn has taught her some of the dances, how to link pinkies and do the steps. It is incredibly loud because of the flat ceiling and the wind instruments and the drums, so the dances are taught entirely through gestures and touch. She is laughing. She is dragged along by the circles of dancers. Grandparents, parents, teenagers and small children. There are a few dogs running between threaded legs. M is at the bar.

He says he doesn't dance Fest Noz. How can you be Breton if you don't dance Fest Noz, she asks. It is equally Breton to stand here and drink. In fact, it is very Breton to stand here and drink and watch you dance.

Some of the songs are in Breton. Rozenn knows what some of the lyrics mean because they are famous and she has checked the liner notes of the cassettes of the major bands that perform them. She shouts a translation of the words into K's ear when they take a break to have another drink. Honor, honor to the White and Black. And damn the traitors.

Was it before or during. These are questions of timing. Was it above or underneath or inside. These are questions of location. Are we against each other or near each other. Are we seated or standing. What is something I must do reflexively and what is something the I can steam through. Where do I place the you. How many days in a fortnight. What is a stage. If we are to measure things are they thick or thin, narrow or wide, full or empty, weak or strong. If you make me a tea how long should it steep. If there is just one homemade ice cube in the pastis and it is warm outside will it still chill the glass. Is the fact you never wear sunscreen going to threaten your life. Will your smoking. Am I too sedentary. Are you sliding into bed with me or are you diving in. Is your sex hard or firm. Am I under an impression or many. Is this a formal or informal question if there is no addressee. Are you sure about this. Does it make any sense. I will have to go to high school again. I will have to sit at desks when I am told. I will forget many of the things we said. You will still be working outside each day. In the winter you will wear an old sailor's sweater with patches on it. You will work uncomplainingly in the earth. I can understand why. I will see a version of you again many times when I travel and meet men who are what one calls salt of the earth. Grounded. Hard men with hard muscles. You drink and you shout and you might lose teeth in a fight. The same men who show me the spider's nest, the beehive, the just-hatched poussins.

You must know that I am always passing through cities and towns and fields with a heavy suitcase full of books and that I make notes and pile up wine bottles outside the house I am renting to write in.

Now you say that there is something strange about a woman who has no children. You tell me I will have them, must have them even when I say that I don't want them.

I am here in Ardmore. On the beach I sit down next to families and lovers and listen. I compare what is said here and now to what I have said to my family and lovers, including you.

This is a grave act of comparison in which I set down these things to be put over and under and against and near and through the rest of what has been said about love, and the world, and their endings.

It is where I do things both reflexively and steaming ahead from the I. It is where I place the you and where I measure the two weeks we had left. It is a stage in life, or a phase if you like. It is thick and thin, narrow and wide, full and empty, weak and strong. It is the tea or pastis you would make me if I came to you now and saw what had happened to you after the constant sun and smoking and you saw me, less lithe and more laden. It is as if I might slide or dive into a bed hard and firm with many impressions culminating in one. It is a formal question asked informally in a language you don't speak, so I suppose it is not addressed to you at all. I am sure about this. It does make sense. I will sit at desks and no one will tell me to.

I have to remember.

*

Sophie has taken the stagiaires to do karaoke. This is an outing to a bar that is sanctioned by the Program. It has been noted in the calendar of activities since their arrival. Some of them, the ones whose parents have completed the form, are allowed one drink. K is not allowed a drink. Sophie encourages them to sign up to sing. The difficulty is that they must sing songs in French, and none of them know any French pop songs. Sophie says she will get up there and help them if needed.

This is all an attempt at introducing them to French bars in a safe and supervised way. It is thought to be particularly important because some of them are staying with families with elderly parents or adults who have no children and so they have not been exposed to what young French people would normally experience. K has been to the festivals, the bars, the car race, and the nightclub. She doesn't want to be here on a Friday at five o'clock doing karaoke with her fellow Americans. She wants to be home checking the tide and waiting for M to return.

He told her it was completely crazy, going to do karaoke at five o'clock in a big group like that. No one will be there and no one will be drunk enough for it to work. She told him it isn't optional. It is part of the cultural programming. Unless she is sick, she must go. He told her to say she is unwell and he will pick her up on his way home and take her up the coast for dinner somewhere. It is too suspicious. Only Jacqueline or Armel can take her home if she is sick during the school day. If it's at the end of the day, no procedure is stated and she would have to ask there on the spot. If he comes, they will ask him questions. She is sure Sophie will detect it.

Sophie is the same age as M. K imagines what it would be like to kiss Sophie and be naked and close to her tiny frame, what it would be like to have her as a lover. What would it be like if Sophie was focus of the story instead M. What if she and Sophie had come together and had had to conceal it.

The stagiaires look young and American. They have all worn their best clothes and the girls are wearing make-up and have smooth hair. The boys have no muscles or solidity. Even the athletic ones are misshapen, unevenly developed. Taken together in a big group everyone looks younger, more American, more out of place. There is an excess of pressed khaki, of white Nikes, of crucifix necklaces, of waterproof jackets and oversized backpacks. K had thought this would have passed by now, that after so many weeks they would all emerge, transformed, each with a new posture and presence. Instead, any attempts they have made to become individuals are lost in the context of the group. They are an undifferentiated blob of Americanness.

The whole bar has been booked. There are no patrons other than these French-speaking American teenagers. The bar staff serve them mainly Cokes. K looks down at her boots, her Tri Yann T-shirt, the scarf tied around her wrist, his triskele at her neck. It is like a costume, a silent karaoke. From the start she had imagined herself to be different from the others, someone special and mythic. Remarkable. That is why he is with her, after all. The other girls wouldn't have drawn him to them. It's her. Her, and the myth she is making. That has to be how she got assigned to this family, the only one with a son in his twenties and a house on a cliff.

*

It was Madame Tanner who did the matching of stagiaires with families. In the interview Madame Tanner must have noted her poetic sensibility despite her technically correct answers to bland questions about quotidian life. The questions were designed to stretch the applicants' vocabulary, to lead them toward certain verb tenses, so the topics were various, but boring. At the end of the interview there was a question about ambitions, future plans. She did not say poet. She did not say she wanted to leave America permanently. She said something about literature and being open to what she is drawn to after finishing college. She said she wanted to live abroad, for a while.

Perhaps this karaoke bar is full of girls like her, but they wear different clothes and do not tell the story of themselves to themselves as it is happening and speculate on the symbolism of common occurrences as related to literary allusions and archetypes. Nor do they look at the past and try to match it up with a concept of a well-written life. They are not writing their autobiography as they go along. If she is remarkable, it could be in this embarrassing and overwrought way. She doesn't sign up to sing.

I was troubled. It was difficult to imagine you sitting down to write me letters. I had known this from the moment I arrived. The house had few books, little paper. There was no sense of pausing, of giving an account of the day or the shape of time passed. In this house on the cliff, everyone worked or learned and returned and rested and took pleasure in food, the sea and sex. When something needed to be mailed, it was a bill or a form and it was a distraction from what was most important, coffee and the morning's bread.

I knew you wouldn't write me letters the way I would write you letters. I knew this would affect what happened later. I knew that once my presence was withdrawn I would no longer consume you.

Any letter would contain far more words than we've ever spoken to each other. There would be a simple voice speaking about things without any exchange, touch or gesture, and that voice would be driven by a limited vocabulary and a desire to keep you reading. How to evoke the me that I was when I was there with you, when I said very little and you weren't saying much either and that was part of the point.

The language of these letters would need to create the shape of that body between us or around us, a body that held us. The language we used then was not part of that body. It came and it went but it did not make it. The only time language entered was when you called me whore, goddess, poet, professor, genius, little silly girl-child. Those words built some of the third body between us, but once listed here, these words do nothing. This is not a popular idea. Love is meant to transcend the bodily presence of the other, especially in language. This is apparently what language is for. Nevertheless, you do not use language the way I use language. Or so I lead myself to believe. Here and now and then, before, during and after and inside your self.

Once I was gone I was gone from you, for you.

You live in language for me at the root of my poetic sensibility so how can you ever be fully gone from me, for me.

This here will never work, though what I want it to work for or toward was unclear to begin with.

To write you a letter I would be veering from embodiment to embodiment, from whore to goddess, professor, poet, genius, silly girl-child. But then I must remember that these were not your words. I put them in your mouth. You read them in my books and in my posturing. The words I would use in any letter I might write would bring together all those words you saw in me, the words you gave me, the words I took, the words I found and claimed for myself.

I lay these words around myself and light them like candles in old shrines. I bring them into my little bedroom, blue for Rimbaud, rose for Baudelaire. Those words taken out of context are the ones that created my body, our body.

So it should come as no surprise there were very few letters from you in the end and that most often they were enclosed with notes and cards from the whole family and photographs of your land and of the horse you bought to rehabilitate. Anyone could read these letters and not feel embarrassed or disturbed. They are official testimonies of affinity and activity. There is no rending of garments or gnashing of teeth because you do not use language in that way, or so I thought.

You still will not or cannot contact me despite all the methods available. Your friend passed my thoughts to you on social media. Links to Breton songs, a description of my life. A poet.

Toujours fidèle à Arthur Rimbaud, as your mother Jacqueline said to me in a recent message.

They have gotten up early on the Saturday morning and driven to the coast of pink granite. None of the others have come with them. They stop off at all the lookouts and take photographs of each other. He takes one of her in front of the famous little house surrounded on both sides by overbearing rocks. She takes one of him, close up, leaning with both arms on a split-rail fence. They hold hands. They eat mussels cooked in cider for lunch and he shows her how to use an empty shell in place of a fork to remove the next body. She wants to go to a hotel and spend the day in bed together. She tells him this and he laughs. You are never satisfied he says. It is a romantic day on the coast and look at you, seventeen and never enough sex for you. What will you be like when you are thirty.

She has two more weeks, less than that, she has ten days. She tells him this. You are right he says but there are no hotels available. It is summer and everyone is here. The paths and streets are packed with couples and families. Ice cream sellers and souvenir stands selling tins of Breton biscuits and red Jacques Cousteau caps.

I will have to take you somewhere in the trees. And you will have to be quiet.

I am already nostalgic for when I wrote these passages Ardmore, Paris, Rennes, Saint-Brieuc.

The ones you have read, not the ones that have been removed.

It is her last night. M is taking her to a party down by the coast. She has spent the day sightseeing with Jacqueline and Rozenn. Classes are optional on this, the final day, and many of the stagiaires' families have taken the day off work to create a final experience for their charges. Jacqueline and Rozenn take her to see the faïences workshops in Quimper. They return to Saint-Brieuc via the forest of Huelgoat where Merlin was imprisoned and died. K and Rozenn had bought red Jacques Cousteau hats in Quimper and wore them into the forest. They climbed on the boulders and posed for photos. An old lady remarked to Jacqueline that she has very beautiful daughters, both with thick hair.

M is at work. K waits for him to arrive home and take her to the party. Tomorrow she will leave and stay for a week in a Parisian convent with the other stagiaires. She will share a room with three girls instead of a bed with M. She will walk in the footsteps of Beauvoir, Beckett, Baudelaire and Duras. She will go to their graves with flowers. She will bring the three girls with her. They will each put a rose in their hair and leave pens and coins on the graves. She will take rubbings of the names on tissue paper for her notebook. There will be photos of her standing in front of each one. She will wish she could meet all the people who left the worn stones carried there from far off places.

M tells her to dress warmly for the party. They will be outside under the stars and it has been a clear day. The wind will come from the north. Jacqueline tells him to make sure to bring K back. The whole family will be disgraced if she is not at the coach tomorrow at noon. There have already been tears in the classes among the students who don't want to go back, who are afraid of speaking English again and becoming someone else. Other students are silent. They are the ones who can't wait to go home and speak English. K thinks they are probably right, were probably right all along. They have not lived in a way that will mean that everything in their futures will never be as vital as this so now they have a possible life to lead. For her, the sea will never be so blue, the sun so warm, the language and love so strong, so simple. Everything has become clear and eternal. Maybe the other students were correct. Maybe this kind of clarity should come later in life. Maybe she will burn herself right out because of this and be forever disappointed.

They arrive at the party in a ramshackle house that emerges like a shipwreck from the sea grass. M introduces her to all his friends, men and women in their twenties who are impressed with her French, for an American especially. They are even more pleased to hear about all the concerts she has been to, and the festivals. They tell M that he has done a good job making her into a Bretonne, and this makes them all laugh. She wonders if she is merely a good story about the time M had an American girl for the whole summer. She doesn't think this can be true but maybe he has given them this impression. He holds her hand and stays close to her. They roast meat directly on the fire and there is a table piled with breads. They drink cider and beer from mugs and the bottles themselves. She thinks she could live here with these people. They could become her friends. She could take a small job teaching English. She'd be able to get one, even now. She could be the one who disappeared into Brittany with her 4.0 GPA and scholarship offers. She could dump her certificates and medals and offer letters into the sea.

They all cheer the setting sun.

K and M drive back to Saint-Brieuc. They listen to her favourite songs on the tape deck. *Tri Martolod, La Blanche Hermine, Dans les prisons de Nantes.* They can barely stay awake. They stop and climb in the back. They make love to stay awake and because they are running out of time. He stops himself. She wants them to get back to her bed. She tells him so. When they reach Saint-Brieuc he turns off toward the Plage du Valais.

She tells him she wants to go back to the house. Dawn is approaching. They are running out of time.

She feels like crying. She is very close to it. He reaches under the seat and pulls out a bottle. Now, for your final morning. It is a bottle of chouchen. The sun is rising over the sea. It tinges the honey liquid pink.

They drink leaning against the car. They are cold and hungover already.

He holds her and kisses her and tells her all of this is hers. All of time is hers and it is not running out at all. Eternity, it is the sea mixed with the sun. Rimbaud.

And this poem.

> *J'ai embrassé l'aube d'été.*

And this poem.

> *Un soir, j'ai assis la Beauté sur mes genoux – Et je l'ai trouvée amère.*

And my reply.

I too kissed the summer's dawn. I laid beauty across my knees.

I saw she was me. I did not find her bitter, or if I was, it was only the taste of the sea.

You read my books when I fell asleep. You inserted their lines into conversation though you claimed to not like or understand poetry. You were the one who used poems to govern our time together.

How could I not have noticed this until now?

She tells him it is impossible for her to leave. They must hide in the forest of Huelgoat.

They drink more and more until the bottle is nearly empty. This is the drink that he said can make even old Breton sailors walk backwards.

The people from the party seem so far away from her now. They have lives here and she does not. K and M leave his car at the sea and climb up the cliff and find his land. Anything seems possible. They are down on the dewy grass. This once. This one time. This once that is the last time.

Her throat and the insides of her elbows tingle. She is a doll that's been taken out of the box and played with vigorously. But she must be returned to the store. She will soon be put back inside the cardboard and plastic. Her hair will be smoothed and her clothes will be folded and rolled and taped and put back in too. White twist-ties will secure her onto the cardboard display at the wrists, ankles, hips and neck. Then she will look the same as before and her eyes will close as she lies back.

I am on a balcony overlooking the sea in Ardmore. The oldest Christian site in Ireland, it was founded by St Declan, St Ailbhe, St Ibar and St Ciaran. I have been walking along a cliff path each day past two looks-outs, one from the Second World War and one from the Napoleonic Wars. I have held the round tower close to my body as I once held yours. I have lain in the grass of the cemetery as I laid in the grass on your land. I have listened to all your music and I have transcribed the words again.

I have been writing with Duras, MD, as my guide. I have just finished *L'Amant* and just reached the same number of words found in that book. It happened somewhere a few pages ago.

I am not certain that this is worth anything, even to me. I wonder how to translate it for you, or to begin to make it clearer in the language it's in. A language that is spoiled, polluted with my thoughts which have been translated, and then not, into another language and back again.

Or perhaps more symbolism is what's needed.

When I reach St Declan's holy well tonight, which is my last night here, I will circle it. I will make the necessary gestures so that this world might reach something of that time, our time, again.

Here in Ardmore jellyfish are building up and the sun is getting stronger. These are not good signs. The Fourth of July was yesterday and there were tanks on the Mall in Washington D.C.

I am listening to the conversations on the beach, at the

holy well, in the five-star restaurant on the cliff. Conversations invoking angles of incidence, angles of attack. Light. Air. Lift. A photograph.

The sun. The sea. Eternity.

My device notifies me it is too hot and cannot be used until it cools down. My device is only for emergencies, like my English-French dictionary once was.

There is no trace in these statements of what you did for me using the words of others. You made statements about me. *Tu m'entoures de ces mots.* You made me into my own myth and I am forever comparing myself to it. *Je participe à ce processus. J'en témoigne, toujours.*

I can still hear the birds.

Yesterday I saw a seal. At first I thought it was a buoy. There were children climbing the cliff face, boys and girls, with all the necessary ropes and knowledge. They sat and listened to instructions and they cheered each other on.

I put on my headphones and clicked the man with that voice and that harp. First I must listen to an advertisement about how to write a novel. It has loud, pounding music. When I click Skip I am permitted to listen, to return to those terrible and gorgeous songs, and the old pain of knowing you and knowing I would be leaving you. I sink into the sound, which is really just a series of changes in air pressure that have come to mean a whole lot.

In Neolithic caves like Newgrange here in Ireland, it has been shown that despite their depth and stone and earth construction, the people conducting ceremonies inside the tomb at night would most certainly have been able to hear the river, even though it was miles away. The dead they were tending would also have been in the presence of these meaningful changes in air pressure.

The strain of the plucked string and the voice that I hadn't expected to move me so, neither the first time I heard it and certainly not again and again.

The man's voice and the harp played in 1972, then on your cassette in 1997 and now on my computer in 2019.

Everything is in working order.

I am obliterated. I return to it again and again.

I have not heard these songs since I packed away the cassette you gave me somewhere in my parents' basement. After I finished my Bachelor's degree, I stopped dragging you around with me.

You never danced at the Fest Noz. You were always at the bar speaking to the old men and watching me and Rozenn circle around. When I returned to Brittany three years later, I learned some Breton at the university in Rennes. I hitched a ride deep into the countryside to a Fest Noz like the small ones you used to take me to. I spoke to an old man at the bar with my Breton and he replied in a way I could understand. Then we talked about Breton in French. Why would an American learn Breton, he said. It is simply unbelievable.

That night I kept searching for you in the crowd though I already knew you were with another girl in Saint-Brieuc.

You were not in this myth, the one I was living at a Fest Noz deep in the countryside where I used my ten words in another new language.

I was there for you.

Their hair has accumulated in the corners of the room. It has mixed with their fingernails, half-moons clipped in the night. When they are clipped one always flies away. The traces of his smell on the leather of the triskele necklace, in the army shirt from his year of national service. She asked him to sleep in her bed for those final hours on the last night when they returned from the field. Now the triskele is around her neck and his blue army shirt is rolled up in her bag. She will wear it every night in the convent in Paris.

Outside the window the tide retreats.

She has his triskele around her neck and his shirt in her suitcase, which is carried downstairs and loaded into the car. The drive to the coach feels like a cortège.

I have not written this story before although I always knew I would.

There is no catastrophe or explosion. There is only evocation, the slow accumulation of time, of tastes and decisions. We say things like 'that moment changed my life' or 'that summer changed my life' when in fact every moment, every summer, does this. Some moments and summers do change things quantifiably more, of course, but I was always going to have a time abroad that changed my life. I was always going to leave Indiana, speak other languages and fill out strange forms, bureaucratic or poetic.

The parts of the summer that could not be guaranteed.

The sex, the love, with him specifically, and with him as someone who could make love without reflection. The house on the cliff could not be guaranteed, nor the Breton nationalism that ran through it. Nor the sun nor the sea.

My Norwegian friend Fredrik says that every time I come to Europe I blow up my life, changing lovers and lives. Fredrik smiles when he says this. Twice I did it in France, once in Spain. Different countries, lovers of different nationalities, always a hope that the destruction of anything too familiar and comfortable will blow me towards the core. Or is it away from the core.

I live here now, on the edge of Europe. It is familiar, comfortable, and not often explosive.

To reach it I have taken a slower route, rappelling down a cliff to the sea.

There is the question of plot and tension. The tension in a love story usually relies on whether the lovers will get together, and once together, whether they can stay together despite a particular challenge or set of challenges put in their way. A challenge for you in reading this is that you know the lovers will get together, it is clear from the start. It is also clear that the lovers will not stay together, despite there being no significant challenge preventing them from doing so had they truly wished to.

Yet perhaps love stories shouldn't hide the fact that most of the time it is possible for lovers to stay together – there being few challenges aside from natural and manmade disasters, war, extreme social penalties and death to truly thwart their staying united. The realm of romance needn't exclude the 'but they didn't's. They had all this: the heights of ecstasy, a simplicity of interaction that seems like a blurring of boundaries between self, other, the earth and cosmos – but they didn't. We didn't. Why is that?

This is a very simple story of summer and sex and language and the sea. Is there a single point in the tale at which it is certain the lovers will not come back together? There is the end of that summer and the meeting once again three years later when he is with someone else. But is that the end?

In fact, any point of this story is where I begin.

I tie this up. I tie you up. She ties him up. She becomes. I am. *Celle qui sait vous garrotter.*

*

It is not clear to her where the rest of the family is. The grandparents, the aunts and uncles, cousins. They don't seem to exist or be nearby. The family of five, now six, seems to be its own universe on the edge of a cliff. And so there are no funerals. Last summer in Indiana there were three. K had almost packed her black Ann Taylor dress, her summer uniform, into the large green suitcase.

Her mother's second eldest sister had visited during that funereal summer. On Saturday, K and her mother and aunt drove to the park they used to visit when she and her brother were children. They were going to hike for a while then go to the nearby antique malls. On their way through the villages and towns, they passed three weddings spilling out from churches. The churches were each different though none of them looked like a typical church. One was a derelict shopping mall, one a clapboard house, another, a purpose-built mega-church. The wedding parties wore brightly coloured dresses and large boutonnieres. One of the wedding receptions, the clapboard house wedding, was a barbeque. The smell of smoke and cooking meat filled the car. Her aunt explained that it's good luck to see weddings and today they have seen three. K wonders if this offsets the funerals.

When she returns to Indiana from Saint-Brieuc, she is taken to the wedding of a couple she doesn't know. Her friend Jen from high school and her parents bring her to this wedding of one of Jen's mother's former students to a Frenchman. They thought it would be fun for K to speak French with the family. That and the family don't speak much English and there are so few French speakers in the area so K's presence is kind of a wedding gift. K meets the couple. They look like male and female versions of each other. Both have long blond hair. Hers is loose under her crown of flowers and his is in a ponytail. K greets them in French and explains why she is there. They are grateful. She wonders what it took to make this happen, for this young woman to get this Frenchman to marry her, for her to be connected forever to the language and the people. Have they even gone to college? K is supposed to be with someone who has gone to college. M has not gone to college. She wonders what this couple will do for work in Indiana. Why would they live here. What is here for them.

The groom says to K, My aunts and great aunts, they are the most lost, please help them understand.

After I left Saint-Brieuc, M moved in with a very young woman whose parents had a house in the neighbourhood, a second home. She was not Breton. She was from Dijon. Her family was rich. They had an extra house in Brittany for the sea and sun. I don't know anything about how M and this young woman came together or quite when it happened. I do know that she was blonde and young, and that she smoked as much as he did. On the evening of my return to Saint-Brieuc, I went to their house with her to wait for M to come home from work. Jacqueline had suggested it.

I was waiting for M, not like before. We were having whiskeys with Coke and she was smoking. The furniture was designer, from the 1980s. We waited and she asked me questions. She was not at university. She worked as a cashier in the grocery store down the road.

We waited with our drinks and she asked what I was studying in Rennes. French Literature, Comparative Literature, Breton language and civilisation.

It was she who was waiting for him. I was not sunning myself on the tiles in my bikini. I was not the one waiting. We were having what you call girl talk but we weren't actually. That is what people would think, what Jacqueline maybe thought we would do. Compare notes.

He came home. He had mud and grass stains across his clothes and the knees of his jeans were torn. His skin was tougher from three more years of sun and held a mixture of expressions taut against his skull.

We kissed each other on each cheek while she made him

a whiskey.

It's good to see you. Your hair is gone, he said.

I had cropped my hair like Winona Ryder. I had on big earrings and boots, the Doc Martens I had bought three years before in Saint-Brieuc. I had on a tight black tank top. I was stronger than before. I was twenty. It had only been three years.

The girl from Dijon tells M that he must practice English. She had been trying to.

I spoke some English with her. There was no Pillar. There was nothing to stop me. She couldn't understand what I was saying.

I asked him if he knew English now. No, he said. I know nothing.

I said that's fine. Once again I am here to speak French.

My French was not as good as it was before. It needed rebuilding. I had not started living in it again.

The girl handed M the whiskey.

You see K I wonder if you mind if I take a shower now with E. That won't bother you will it. I would really like it. Relax here with a whiskey, she said.

No, I said. It won't bother me at all.

She took him by the hand and giggled. She pulled him up

the stairs. He looked back at me and smiled.

I sat on the designer couch. I read a magazine and drank whiskey.

Rimbaud's manuscripts are in the cabinet and the staff will not unlock it. K had taken the train from Rennes to Paris and then transferred stations. She had met her Norwegian friend Fredrik in a bar near Gare de l'Est. They each drank four beers and ate free nuts. She boarded the slow train to Charleville-Mézières. She had a letter of introduction from her professor in Rennes. It says she is to be shown the manuscripts, which is unusual for an American undergraduate, but her professor is a well-known nineteenth-century poetry scholar and she is the best student in the class.

The staff tell her the keeper of manuscripts is not on site. The dates are wrong. They thought she was arriving last week. They wondered why she had not come. They do not have the authority to show her the manuscripts. They don't even have a key to this cabinet. But yes, the original manuscripts are in there. That's where they are, if it is any consolation.

They say this as though they know that she wants to absorb some poetic vibrations from the cabinet, as though they too think this is possible.

She tells them that they have a real problem on their hands and that if there was a fire, they would not be able to save the manuscripts because they have no key. If the only person with the key is the keeper of manuscripts then the manuscripts aren't really safe, are they? This is something they should look into immediately, she says. This is a real risk. Look at this cabinet, it doesn't appear to be fire-proof.

This is how she tells them that she knows they have a key

but are refusing to show her because they believe in protocol and pillars and codes. They tell her she can come back another time. They can make a new appointment for her.

She has no money. She is twenty. She will never come back to Charleville. She will never see these manuscripts. She won't be making this trip again. She begins to cry in the archives. They comfort her. They all stare at the cabinet together. That night she drinks in a bar dedicated to Elvis near the Place Ducale. The next day she goes to cemetery where Rimbaud is buried next to his older sister. The sister who died aged seventeen.

Then she leaves for Saint-Brieuc to find M, to meet his new girl.

In the radio interview a scholar of nineteenth-century French literature is asked why no one wants to believe that it is indeed a grown-up Rimbaud who has been photographed on a hotel terrace in Aden. Rimbaud sits with other white men and one pregnant white woman in a place they do not belong, in a place they should not be. We know who the woman is, as well as most of the men. The eventual birth of the baby is recorded in the archive.

Why does no one want to believe it is Rimbaud in this photograph even if it has been ninety percent verified that it is him, there, in Aden, at the centre of the picture, staring straight at the lens.

The scholar says it is unbearable for this to be Rimbaud. No one can stand to see the genius of sixteen to twenty years old who has been immortalised in a grand painting and iconic photographs suddenly a man of thirty, with a moustache, there in Aden, at the edge of the world.

He says Rimbaud is missing his halo.

For years I avoided reading the plain letters Rimbaud wrote to his family after he stopped writing poetry. The letters arrived in Charleville from Cyprus, Harar, Aden, his deathbed in Marseille.

> *I am writing this from the desert and I don't know when we will get going.*
>
> *In the mountains there's nothing but ferns and fir trees.*
>
> *I'm not sending a photograph. I carefully avoid all*

unnecessary expenditure.

I wouldn't reach you until the end July...

The scholar says no one wants to see this man dressed in white linen with a moustache on the hotel veranda looking right at us. They want the precocious child who is the object of Verlaine, who makes the man, Verlaine, his object. We want the child who looks away, somewhere beyond the frame at his next treat or prey. We don't want the man. We especially don't want this man on a veranda in Aden to look at us down the lens. To confront us.

M confronted me in that photo. He looked at me down the lens.

Now M is contacting me, quite suddenly. Through his friend who is on social media. M is not on social media, does not email. I am going to France now to continue writing this. It was already planned. What is this coincidence?

Thirty-nine and forty-four. Zero children and two. Would it be unbearable for you to see our photograph?

The stagiaires are in Paris. They are staying in a convent, four stagiaires of the same sex to a room.

She has told her roommates. She has gotten away with it, all summer. The sea, the sun, and M. The Program can't send her back now.

Today they have free time before they go on the Bateaux Mouches in the evening. They have been encouraged to speak English a bit more each day, but no one is succeeding or really trying. K has set the itinerary and brought her three roommates along. The literary cafés, Montparnasse cemetery, the Catacombs. They have done all of these. They make their way to the Eiffel Tower with baguette sandwiches. The August sun blasts the sidewalk. They all wear jeans with tank tops. In their attempt to look less like American tourists, they have abandoned shorts. She has the scarf wrapped and tied around her wrist, and she uses it to wipe sweat from her forehead. They eat their sandwiches and drink Orangina. K is almost enjoying herself.

Sharing a room, she has not been able to cry since the departure and has turned her focus to hitting all the literary hotspots she had identified before coming to France. The air-conditioned galleries of the Louvre and the Musée d'Orsay, and the sparsely furnished convent have emptied her ears of the sound of his voice and the smell of his skin, though the leather strap of the triskele necklace still contains the faintest trace of his cologne.

In the park Audra sees the man first and tries to describe him and what he is doing. Audra says that man is lying over there with a plastic thing, watching us and rubbing it. Audra struggles to name the plastic thing. She says its colour is like pink flesh. He has been doing it for a while she says. The others strain to see the man among the crowd of picnickers and tour groups. Suddenly they all spot him lying back in the grass with the plastic thing in his hand. It is a fake penis. They have forgotten the word for this in English, some of them have never known it. He is rubbing the penis and looking straight at them.

K says we need to get away from him now.

She is angry. She wants to run toward the man and kick him in the shins and stamp on his face. She doesn't want this man's thoughts and gestures all over her, all over Paris, and all over this summer she has had.

They stand up and put on their backpacks, stuffing the napkins and packaging into their pockets. The man stands up too. He is walking toward them. They can't believe it.

They start running. He runs after them.

As they run K shouts for help.

No one does anything or seems to understand what she is referring to. Now they are well away from the park and he is still chasing them along the pavement. They cross a wide street. There is a tourist kiosk selling Eiffel Tower keychains, postcards, plates. They slide themselves between the racks. The man disappears.

They decide to go to Notre Dame, Shakespeare and Co., and the Beat Hotel. They take the metro part of the way because it's hot. Then they walk along the Seine, stopping at the book stalls. They look at each man they pass, especially the ones who are stationary, sitting on benches or leaning against trees. They wonder which of these men would do that in a park. Who would chase them, who would do something worse.

They find the Beat Hotel in a side street near Notre Dame. There are black and white photographs of the famous writers, all male, along the walls. No longer a flophouse for artists and writers, the lobby's plush chairs are placed carefully in front of the photographs so tourists can pose with them in the background. The receptionist continues typing when they enter.

Audra asks K if she wants her photo taken in the various chairs. Or at the stately desk.

K says no. I've had enough.

They move on to Notre Dame. At the entrance an old man is holding a small white dog under his arm. In his other hand there is small leather pouch with a few coins inside. His shoes are held together with twine. They give him money and their extra bottle of Orangina.

Inside the cathedral the organ is playing. K crosses herself with holy water and lowers herself onto one knee in the direction of the main altar behind which is the body of Christ. The others don't do these things because they are Protestant. She sees a priest and asks him if he can help her to find the reliquary, the one with the crown of thorns. He says it is only shown one day per year and today is not the day.

He points to the confessionals that line the walls. You are welcome to confess your sins, he says.

There are signs outside each wooden booth indicating the languages available in each one.

She tells him no thanks, I am fine.

K is at Café de la Rotonde ordering sole meunière and one glass of white wine, then a coffee. She is wearing the white tank top and purple jeans with the triskele around her neck and the scarf around her wrist. She is wearing the Rose Ispahan perfume M gave her. She has convinced the stagiaires, her friends, to spend the last of their money here after seeing the graves in Montparnasse Cemetery.

K is asking herself whether M would know who Marguerite Duras was. She has taken a rubbing from her grave. Duras, MD, died last year, 1996. K has just missed her.

I return to Paris. I sit down at La Rotonde and order sole meunière and wine, then a coffee. It is on the way from Charleville to Saint-Brieuc, 2000.

I return to Paris. I sit down at La Rotonde and order sole meunière and wine, then a coffee. It is when my mother is in the American hospital in Neuilly in 2013, the hospital where Gertrude Stein died in 1946.

I return to Paris. I sit down at La Rotonde and order sole meunière and wine, then a coffee, and write.

I return to Paris. I sit down at La Rotonde and order sole meunière and wine, then a coffee, and write this.

I am sitting at La Rotonde now. Writing this.

Earlier at Duras's grave a young woman was weeping or trying to weep. A young woman. Weeping or trying to weep. I could not tell.

In Duras's books, especially *L'Amant de la Chine du Nord*, her re-write of *L'Amant*, everyone weeps. Tears are always poised for release.

Writing or rewriting a love story requires emptying the mind of any sense of what love can be or has been, for anyone else as well as for yourself.

This is what is required, but it cannot actually be done.

The green tide has arrived in Saint-Brieuc. Seventeen wild pigs, a jogger and a horse are dead from toxic gases. The skull and crossbones sign on the barrier surrounding the Plage du Valais is weathered along with four years' worth of torn stickers and notices reinstating another summer's closures.

The green algae is nourished with what feeds the farms. For years, only a few such plants existed and it was fine to swim with it floating nearby. Now the algae cannot be controlled. It piles up and rots and releases its lethal poison. The mountains of algae cannot be gathered and destroyed fast enough and so the sea must be closed.

I walked to the beach yesterday, alone. This was before I met you in the centre of town. I walked in the rain all the way from the train station to the coast like an idiot or a spy or a ghost. I crossed over the motorway on the concrete bridge and descended into the valley. I arrived at the scar of the port cutting through the pines and the bar where we drank a beer the day you first took my hand.

I climbed to the ancient tower with its hidden bombs, which is still locked behind gates to protect us. The rain rushing down the steep hill almost took me off my feet. Then I came to the street where you lived, where we all lived. And then to the sea.

The sea was closed.

When I saw you in the bar that evening for the first time in nineteen years you told me that for generations everyone swam in it, in the green algae, the salade.

Yes, I said, I remember it.

We swam in it together, you said.

We swam in the warm sea with the salade, the algae. It floated underwater and caressed our ankles like the softest of hands.

But it's a tragedy, I said. The sea is closed in Saint-Brieuc.

You tell me a truck driver clearing the algae from the beach was overcome by the fumes. Now they don't even try to take it away. They just lock up the sea until winter.

You don't know that I have already written us into the sea, I have written you and me into the sea, here. I do not tell you this. I do not tell you I have just made it all happen again.

We are swimming in the warm sea with the salade, here.

I have ritualised it. I have consecrated it.

In the saying I made it so.

This story isn't anywhere else I've written, not really. It seemed important to locate significant people, significant plot lines.

Perhaps you felt the same when you located me.

In the year after MD learns of the death of her lover, she rewrites their story, the story she had told years before in her most famous book. She prefaces the new version with a note that says her lover's death has produced something unimaginable – rewriting the story has made her a writer of novels once again, in 1991.

This year, as the world is dying like the sea in St-Brieuc, I wrote the story of this young girl and her lover, the story that made me a poet.

Seventeen. The age of hope and fantasy. I am the girl who can tie your hands. When I am very strong, few retreat. As the world winds down to a single dark wood, to a beach, to a house, I have found you.

I have stated my good beliefs, my hopes, my feelings – all those things cherished by poets. I watch the birth of my thoughts. They are clear to me. I examine them. I lean in and listen to them.

And so I am a thousand times richer.

August 2019

ACKNOWLEDGEMENTS

Writing began at the Molly Keane House in Ardmore, Co. Cork, and finished at the Centre Culturel Irlandais in Paris.

Thank you to readers of both early and late drafts – Abi Curtis, Joanna Walsh and Francesca Bratton.

Thank you to Alessio Baldini, Ailbhe Darcy, Amelia DeFalco, Clare Fisher, Anne-Marie Evans, Liam Harrison, Joanne Hayden, Daisy Hildyard, Caleb Klaces, and Tiffany Tondut for encouraging me to write the poet K's adventures in prose.

Thanks to my agent Becky Thomas of Lewinsohn Literary for championing the words I have, and my editor Suze Olbrich for bringing them out so beautifully.

Thank you to Jon Hughes who keeps me going as I pull things together and make things up.

AUTHOR BIOGRAPHY

Professor of Poetry at the University of Leeds, Kimberly Campanello's publications include *MOTHERBABYHOME* (zimZalla, 2019), *sorry that you were not moved* (Fallow Media, 2022) and *(S)worn State(s)* (The Salvage Press, 2024). Her writing has appeared in *Granta*, *The White Review*, *The London Magazine*, *Tolka*, *The Pig's Back*, *Poetry Ireland Review*, *Poetry Review* and *Somesuch Stories*. Her latest poetry collection *An Interesting Detail* is forthcoming from Bloomsbury Poetry. *USE THE WORDS YOU HAVE* is her first novel.

Kimberly Campanello